An Aura of Desperation

1

Jill was trying to walk as subtly as possible because she didn't want to show the telltale signs of desperation that were currently filling her bladder. She was walking with her friends Henry and James, who although they shared her interest in seeing women desperate to pee, she always felt kind of awkward around them when they knew she actually had to go to the bathroom.

That was one of the awkward things about sharing an interest in women desperate to pee. Sure the three of them had a mutual love of the entire topic, but it's different when you are watching others, but being the one watched is kind of awkward. So although Jill would often enjoy watching other women desperate with her two male friends, she would try not to show her own desperation or admit when she had to go to the bathroom if at all possible. She still felt extremely awkward about that.

However as they continued walking around the mall Jill realized you can only put off nature's call for so long. Jill could feel all of that soda that she had drank at lunch quickly filling up her bladder. She figured that her two companions probably also had to go to the bathroom, or would at some point, but maybe they didn't want to say anything because maybe they were equally awkward about admitting needing to go to the bathroom while she was around.

Jill began walking quicker and quicker as they continued walking through the mall.

"Whoa Jill, wait up," Henry said as he and James caught up. "Are you like speed walking or something?"

Jill stopped walking for a moment and turned around to see that her companions were huffing and puffing catching up to her.

"Sorry guys I didn't realize that you couldn't keep up," Jill said. "I don't think that I was power walking but maybe I was walking more quickly than I thought I was."

"Are you eager to get some place in a hurry?" James asked.

"Yeah it looks like you are rushing to get somewhere," Henry said.

"No, nowhere in particular," Jill said as she subtly looked out of the corner of her eye to see the ladies room which as usual had an ever-growing line out the door.

"You seemed like you were going awfully fast for going nowhere in particular," Henry said.

Jill shrugged her shoulders. "No, I just I think there's a new bookstore around here or something like that."

"Are you sure, I don't remember anything about a bookstore here?" James asked.

"I'm pretty sure it's around here somewhere," Jill said as she turned around taking the opportunity to once again glance nonchalantly at the ladies room and its ever-growing line.

"He's right Jill I don't see any type of bookstore around here," Henry said as he looked around. "I think that you were rapidly walking in the opposite direction."

"Maybe we should just ask someone?" James said before he saw the map of the mall. He started looking up and down and found the sign that said you are here where they were stationed not far from the food court. "Which bookstore were you looking for?"

"There's more than one?" Jill asked.

James nodded. "Yep, it shows right here on the map. There are two bookstores in the mall and both of them are in the opposite direction in which you were rapidly jogging."

"How silly of me," Jill said as she bent down a little bit to look at the map using the opportunity to take some of the pressure off of her bladder.

"I guess we should start heading in the opposite direction then," Henry said.

"Well hey we're over in this direction right now, we might as well look around and see what's around here," Jill said once again trying to look as subtly as possible at the ladies room. But she saw that there was a huge line and that there was no way she could use it discreetly without them obviously knowing and without seeing her waiting in that line for probably 20 or 30 minutes.

"Well I know what's around here," James said as he looked towards the bathroom.

"You do?" Jill said sounding nervous.

"Yeah I majorly have to take a piss," James said as he

laughed.

"Me too, all that stuff we drank at lunch really goes through you fast doesn't it," Henry said.

"I'll just wait here a minute," Jill said as she watched James and Henry walk into the empty men's room. She looked at the ladies room and saw that there was no way she was getting in quickly and although she didn't like to do it she decided to go to the front of the line and tap a woman on the shoulder. "You don't suppose I could cut you in line do you?"

"Absolutely not, my bladder is ready to explode," the woman said.

Jill looked up and down the line to see lots of frowning and distressed looking faces and she bit her lip. She would really like to go to the bathroom but she didn't feel like waiting in line for a half hour while Henry and James got a free show. There was nothing more embarrassing than being the focus of everyone's attention when your bladder was about to explode.

Jill waited outside of the bathroom and it seemed like only a minute or two had gone by before Henry and James came out with big smiles on their faces.

"Take care of everything?" Jill said raising her eyebrows.

"Yep, never a line at the men's room," James said with a boisterous laugh.

"You really like to rub that in don't you," Jill said.

"When I think about it I like to rub one out," Henry said as he and James high-fived each other.

"Shall we get going," Jill said. Every instinct in her body said that she should get in line right now but she certainly wasn't going to do that while Henry and James were there and stand there for a half hour as they gawked at her. That was one of the perils of having to opposite sex friends who share your particular interest in seeing members of your sex desperate to go to the bathroom. At some point you are going to be among them and it's much more fun to view others than it is to be viewed yourself.

The three of them began walking away and a little voice in the back of Jill's head said that she should get in line right then and there but she wasn't yet at the level of an emergency. Sure she really had to go, but she wasn't about to admit that to others.

"Hey I wonder how many of those women waiting in line are

at the stage where they are completely bursting and desperate," Henry said.

"Yeah it would be great to know just how badly every woman in line had to go to the bathroom," James said.

"Well Einstein, there is sort of a simple assumption that you can make," Jill said as the three of them stopped and stood there.

"What exactly is that?" Henry asked.

"Well they might not all be desperate to the point where they're ready to explode," Jill said. "But consider it this way, if they are already waiting in line for the bathroom they obviously feel like they have to go bad enough that they aren't going to wait any longer, and knowing that there would likely be a line they didn't want to take any chances."

"You know that makes perfect sense," Henry said. "But not all bladders were created equal. Some of these women certainly must have to go a lot more than others and they aren't necessarily at the front of the line so to speak."

"Well I guess that's what makes desperation interesting isn't it, we're not all on the equal playing field," Jill said desperately wanting to cross her legs but not wanting to be obvious.

"Yes some of us can pee without having to wait for an hour," James said as he once again high-fived Henry.

Jill shook her head once again. "You really do love rubbing it in don't you?"

"Hey Jill don't be angry just because you are jealous," Henry said. "We're all female desperation fans here."

"Yes we all enjoy female desperation, although two of us enjoy it strictly from an observational standpoint," Jill said.

"Works for us," Henry and James said in unison as they began laughing.

"Look I love seeing women squirming for the toilet as well but at some point everyone is going to have to go to the bathroom just like her fellow sisters and that is the point at which the enjoyment of simply watching ends and the practical need to get to a bathroom begins," Jill said.

"Yeah but is there any specific telltale signs that a woman is ready to explode?" Henry said. "Come on Jill use your insider knowledge to let us know which of these women in line is probably suffering the most bladder pain."

Jill had to admit that frankly this was not what she wanted to be thinking about at the moment as the tingling feeling in her bladder grew more intense by the moment. But she took a deep breath and tried her best not to show it.

"Well sometimes desperation can be really subtle," Jill said, ironically enough just bending her knees very slightly and nonchalantly. "It may surprise you to learn that most women don't want to be dancing around like a maniac and announcing to the world that their bladder is about to explode. Most women want to try and maintain some decorum and not to seem like a raving lunatic who can't think about anything other than the pressure building about to explode in her bladder!" Jill realized that they were staring at her. "At least that's what it's like I think for most women. Plenty of women show lots of obvious signs."

"Who in this line do you think is the most desperate?" James asked.

Jill looked up and down the line and she saw lots of frowning faces, lots of eyes looking ahead to the front of the bathroom, a couple of people looking outside of the line almost wanting to step out of the line and a couple more who seemed to be very subtly crossing and uncrossing their legs. One woman seemed to be tapping her heel very quickly and looking impatient.

"Well if you look at the woman tapping her heel you can see that she is highly impatient," Jill said fighting the instinct to tap her own heel. "That doesn't necessarily mean that she is the most desperate but it means that she is probably the most aggravated and is making subtle motions to try and take her mind off of her bladder.

"Then you can see lots of women who are sort of stepping outside of the line and trying to look at the head of the line to see how many people are in front of them, which suggests that they are probably growing more frantic by the moment.

"Then there is that woman towards the front of the line who is obviously pregnant so she is probably worse off than most, and if I were her I would probably try to play upon people and their sympathy and hope that maybe they will let me cut in line.

"You can also see that most of the women in line or at least some of them are crossing and uncrossing their legs. So like I said probably most of them have to pee badly enough that they can't put off the need any longer and can't ignore the need and that it's very obvious."

"Wow those are some pretty good observations," James said as he and Henry nodded. "You really are an expert at this Jill. How did you learn all this stuff?"

Jill raised her eyebrow again. "Really, you really actually have to ask that? Let me just sum it up like this, live and learn gentlemen, live and learn."

As they stood there observing the line Jill had to admit it was fun seeing these women squirming for the bathroom but it was also making it harder to suppress and ignore her own growing desire to relieve herself. She knew that the guys wanted to stay and watch the line for a while but they were trying to be discreet about it. However after a few moments that woman at the front of the line who Jill had asked to cut earlier walked out of the room and gave her a look as she saw the two guys standing next to her and laughing.

"I think that that woman was kind of giving you the stare down Jill," Henry said. "Do you know her?"

Jill shrugged her shoulders. "I haven't the foggiest clue." Jill looked at the woman walking away with a more easy-going stride and Jill pretty much wanted to trip her, except if she did so the woman's bladder would be empty so it wouldn't be as dramatic. "We probably shouldn't stay around and stare, we will look kind of out of place with you guys around especially."

"Hey don't pretend that you're not enjoying watching as well," Henry said.

"Yes but if you're not actually waiting in line you should probably only take subtle looks," Jill said. "Anyway I really wanted to check out those bookstores so why don't we go down that way?"

As Jill started rapidly walking in the direction of the bookstores and away from the bathrooms she had to admit that that little voice in the back of her head, her female intuition perhaps, was telling her that she was going in the wrong direction. In fact that little voice in her head was probably the voice of her bladder screaming out for some relief. But she also didn't want to let on that she had to go to the bathroom.

It took them a while to get to the bookstore despite the fact that Jill was pretty much sprinting there. She tried looking at the books and magazines to take her mind off of her bladder but she couldn't help but try crossing and uncrossing her legs subtly. She tried to be as nonchalant about it as possible and she was surprised that even after the lecture she gave that the guys were not picking up on it.

Jill you're a master of subtlety, she thought right before the ache in her bladder reminded her how badly she had to go to the bathroom. She had no idea how she was going to sneak off and be able to use the bathroom quickly and felt like at some point she would probably have to bite the bullet, get in line for the bathroom and there wasn't anything she could do about that.

As Jill and the guys were walking around to the bookstore in the magazine section Jill couldn't help but notice a rather heavyset girl who was crossing her legs in a similar manner and she could even see that the girl subtly grabbed herself when no one was looking.

"What are you looking at Jill?" Henry said as he and James looked forward.

"See that girl over there with the magazine subtly crossing her legs, I saw her grab herself a moment ago, she definitely has to pee," Jill said shaking her head.

"You can tell even when she's not in line for the bathroom?" James asked.

"Hey let's be quiet, we don't want to seem creepy and weird," Jill said.

"Let's go over and talk to her," Henry said.

"Go talk to her, and say what?" Jill said very discreetly bending at the knees a little bit. "It's not like we can go up to her and say hey do you have to pee?!"

"That's true," James said. "Although it seems like a perfect opportunity to talk to a desperate girl."

"You wouldn't know a desperate girl if she bit you," Jill said as she pictured herself biting James and laughing, in fact she started laughing out loud at the fact that James and Henry seemed still oblivious to the fact that she had to go to the bathroom, despite the fact that she drank as much as they did and has been walking around the mall with them all this time. Luckily Jill was a master of stealth.

"What are you laughing at Jill?" James asked.

"Nothing, it's an inside joke, you wouldn't get it," Jill said. "Hey where did that girl go?"

"Excuse me," a voice said behind them and they all turned

around to see the girl from before standing there.

"Oh hi," Jill said. "You startled me."

"My name's Chelsea, I really need the bathroom so I really hate to ask a stranger this, but do you have any idea where the ladies room is?" Chelsea said. "I have looked all around the mall and I haven't found it all day and it's really easy to get lost in places like this."

"It's true they really do hide the bathrooms around here," Jill said as suddenly a light bulb went off in her head. "Hey why don't I show you where the bathroom is?" Now she could go over to the ladies room and the guys would be none the wiser.

"Hey we will go with you," Henry said, immediately sinking Jill's spirits.

"Hey you guys you know it's kind of far away, I can take care of this," Jill said raising her eyebrows again trying to signal to them that this was sort of a woman thing. "You can just stay here in the bookstore and I will meet up with you later. You guys will probably be here for a while right?"

"Okay Jill," James said. "We will be right here waiting for you."

Jill could practically burst with joy over the fact that her evil little plan worked. Although her bladder could burst from being too full, so she hoped to get over to the bathroom quickly.

"Thanks for escorting me to the ladies room personally," Chelsea said. "You really didn't have to do that."

"Oh no I really did, think nothing of it," Jill said as she was walking rather quickly.

"Hey slow down, I don't want to lose you," Chelsea said. "You don't have to rush on my account." That was when Chelsea smiled and looked at Jill. "Oh I see what's going on here."

"You do," Jill said suddenly wondering what was going through Chelsea's head.

"I can see that you are crossing your legs right now," Chelsea said as she laughed and Jill joined in.

"Guilty, I have to go, quite bad actually," Jill said. "And I would rather the guys I am with not know that I am sneaking off to the bathroom. In fact you actually gave me the perfect pretext to make a discreet visit to the ladies room without anyone being none the wiser."

"I guess you aren't as altruistic as I thought," Chelsea said as she laughed. "But hey when you help someone they should help you. And I totally get what you mean about not wanting the guys to know that you have to go to the bathroom; it is super embarrassing isn't it?"

"Okay let's get our asses to the bathroom and onto those toilet seats because there was quite a line when I left before!"

"There always is," Chelsea said as the two of them began power walking their way to the ladies room to find that the line seemed to be even longer. Chelsea got in line ahead of Jill and Jill enjoyed this because she got some good view of Chelsea doing the telltale signs of the pee dance, although at the same time she kind of wished that she was first in line because she would be going to the bathroom quicker in that case.

"It seems like you have to go pretty bad," Jill said.

"Those large sodas go right through you; I can't believe I didn't notice this bathroom when I came by the food court before."

"Hey it's easy to miss, it's like they are trying to purposely hide the ladies rooms around here."

For the next couple of minutes Jill and Chelsea made small talk and luckily the line was going surprisingly fast, although still as slow as molasses for anyone who has to go as badly as they did. Finally they were at the front of the door that would at least lead them into the restroom and Jill felt like she was really going to make it.

"Oh thank God it's almost our turn," Chelsea said barely able to stand still anymore.

"Amen to that," Jill said but then she saw the last thing in the world that she wanted to see. It was James and Henry off in the distance walking over to them. "Crap I can't let them see me in line."

Jill was practically ready to scream but she got out of the line and started walking towards Henry and James.

"What took you so long Jill?" Henry said. "We got worried and decided to come looking for you."

"Nothing," Jill said looking at the bathroom and her place in line that she had now abdicated.

"Where did Chelsea go?" James said.

"Oh I just thought that I should probably wait for her to make sure she got back to the bookstore safely," Jill said as she looked at the entrance to the bathroom and saw Chelsea walking towards them.

"Hey Jill where did you go," Chelsea said as she came over with a smile and look of relief on her face as she walked over with a confident stride.

"Oh I was just waiting out here for you like I said I would," Jill said as she gave Chelsea a look as she nodded.

"Oh I got you," Chelsea said as she winked back and her smile looked even wider than before as she seemed to have realized that Jill did not get the chance to use the bathroom. "So hey would you like to go see the water fountain where you can throw the coins in?"

Jill wanted to say something but the pain in her bladder was becoming overwhelming. Was Chelsea toying with her? "You know I think I'm good," Jill said looking to the front of the ladies room where she was just a moment ago.

"Are you sure Jill?" Chelsea asked.

Jill didn't want to do it but she knew that she could not walk away from the bathroom. At the same time she didn't want to admit that she was ready to explode.

"Something the matter Jill?" Henry asked.

Control yourself Jill, Jill said to herself.

"Yeah don't you want to see the water fountain," James said. "With all that loud spouting water?"

Finally Jill could take it no more. "Screw it!" she said as she walked to the front of the bathroom line. "I just got out of line for a moment but do you think I could get back in line now?"

Everyone gave Jill the stare down and shook their heads as she slinked to the back of the line.

Henry, James and Chelsea all burst out laughing. Jill couldn't help but join in, not because she thought that it was funny the situation that she was in, but simply because she thought it funny that until she actually said something they hadn't realized that she was bursting.

She was just that good. But now the cat was out of the bag and she would have to endure the next 20 minutes with her head held high and her legs crossed tight. It was going to be a very long 20 minutes.

2

Jill had to admit that she was embarrassed being seen waiting in line by Henry and James. Although they all loved female desperation equally Jill felt that they would probably never understand what it was like from the female perspective, and just how awkward it was to be waiting in line with a full bursting bladder like that. Despite all the times that they enjoyed watching other women in line Jill always felt like she was giving in or putting on a show for them that she would rather not put on whenever she gave into her urge to get in line and go to the bathroom.

While Jill was checking her email and her friends asked if she wanted to go to the local town carnival she had to admit that it sounded fun but she certainly didn't want to go to the bathroom while she was there, so she was going to try and limit her intake of liquids in the hours leading up to the fair that night.

She met up with James and Henry at the fair and it looked like it was a pretty big turnout.

"Wow this is the most crowded I have seen this particular fair in years," Jill said. "Normally it's a pretty low key event but it looks like they went all out this year. Still you can tell that the rides are fairly cheap, the games are probably rigged and I don't know if I would want to try any of the food that they serve here."

"Especially since there aren't any bathrooms," James said.

"What was that," Jill said as she practically did a double take.

"He said that they don't have any bathrooms," Henry said. "I guess it's such a small scale event they didn't think to spring for a porta potties or anything like that."

"Not that anyone really wants to use a porta potty," Jill said. "But still you'd think if they were planning a big public event like this it makes sense to provide toilets, cause what do they expect everyone to do when they have to go to the bathroom?"

"Pee outside," Henry and James said simultaneously and laughed.

"Easier said than done, you guys have penises," Jill said.

"High-five for penises," Henry said as he and James slapped each other five.

"But that's the whole point of coming to a place like this Jill," James said shaking his head and looking around. "Look at all of these women going around at the fair completely oblivious to the fact that when nature calls they will have no place to go."

Jill shook her head. "Still you would think that at any outdoor event like this with so many people who are eating and drinking it would make a good business sense to provide some place to go to the bathroom."

"Well it's a local town fair Jill," Henry said shaking his head. "They probably figured that most of the people are coming here from just a couple of blocks away and just walked here so there isn't really any incentive to provide bathrooms. They probably figured that anyone who has to go to the bathroom bad enough will most likely end up going home."

"The bad thing is that without any place for the women to line up to go to the bathroom there's no way to know that they have to pee," James said. "Which again is the real reason I thought we should all come to this event, I mean unless Jill has to go to the bathroom herself again, which would be hilarious."

"I don't have to go to the bathroom," Jill said. "And once again if I did have to go to the bathroom I don't think that you guys would even notice. As much the connoisseurs as you are of the female desperation world you just are not attuned to the signs of desperation in the way an actual woman is."

The two of them nodded at Jill.

"That's why it's good to have you with us Jill," James said. "You can spot the telltale signs of desperation on women in a crowd in a way that we couldn't. So do you see any women who look like they have to go to the bathroom Jill?"

Jill started scanning the crowd and she noticed a woman with a child who seemed to be jumping up and down at her leg.

"That woman might have to go to the bathroom," Jill said as she pointed to the woman with child. "Actually I think that her child probably has to go to the bathroom from the way she is carrying on."

The woman started walking away with her child who seemed like she was upset.

Jill shook her head. "You know those are some pretty telltale signs that she probably has to go to the bathroom. Unfortunately at a fair like this people probably would just go home when they find the urge to go to the bathroom."

Henry shrugged his shoulders. "Yeah but on the other hand you have to figure that some people have come here from further away than we are and they might have a really long walk to go home, which might incline them to hold it in, so to speak."

James nodded. "He has a good point Jill, he knows what he's talking about."

"You guys don't have to mansplain female desperation to me," Jill said. "As a woman you live with desperation as a major part of your life. Sure it varies from person to person but I can guarantee that every woman if you pry deep enough will have one really juicy situation in which she badly needed a toilet but was unable to find one."

"All of them?" James asked as he looked around at the audience.

Jill nodded and smiled. "Yes, without exception, I would say absolutely every woman has a major desperation experience somewhere in her history. It might be buried down really far and she might not want to talk about it but I can still guarantee that she has a story somewhere."

Henry and James smiled at each other and then high-fived each other again.

"It's too bad we just can't go up to these women and ask them if they have ever had to pee really bad and weren't able to go," James said.

"That would probably be pretty weird," Henry said shaking his head. "But what would be really cool is if there was just some way to know which women were desperate even if they weren't showing any outwardly visible signs of being desperate, like a desperation barometer or something like that."

"If you just observe carefully then I think that you will notice a lot of women are showing the signs of having to go to the bathroom," Jill said as she looked around to see a woman looking at one of those games where you shoot a water pistol into the clown's mouth to start filling up the balloon who was leaning over, and it looked like she had her legs crossed and was shaking a bit.

"You see something Jill?" Henry asked as he looked over in the distance and saw the woman at the game with the clowns and the balloons.

"That woman over there, I think she has to pee," Jill said as she pointed to the woman as she heard the loud hiss of the water pistol going off and balloons popping. Jill had to admit the sound of that hissing water was starting to get to her and that was when she realized in spite of her best efforts she already found that she had to go to the bathroom, which disappointed her because she knew that they would probably be at the fair for several more hours.

The woman at the clown game walked away with a big stuffed panda bear and looked pretty pleased with herself but Jill could see that she seemed to be standing on her heel with her knees slightly bent and her legs noticeably crossed.

"I think Jill's right, that woman does look like she needs to go to the bathroom," James said. "I just really wish that there were some way to know for sure."

"Trust me after playing a game like that if she had to go to the bathroom even a little now she is probably positively bursting," Jill said. "The fact that she was playing with water, the fact that she was looking at balloons filled with water exploding, the fact that she was bending over at an uncomfortable and awkward position for the bladder, all of it is basically screaming the fact that she has to go to the bathroom and probably has to go badly."

"Maybe we could follow her for a while," Henry said." You know very discreetly just to see what happens."

"I have to admit I always feel creepy when we are doing this," Jill said. "There is something about following around a person just because you hoped that their bladder is going to explode that sounds like more than even a stalker, it just sounds really weird and creepy."

"You're probably overthinking this too much Jill," Henry said. "Now we all came here to see desperate women and I personally think that now that we finally found one to lose the trail would make us bad hunters."

"Okay even I have to agree that when you refer to it as hunting it does almost sounds kind of stalker-ish," James said.

"Are you saying that you don't want to follow around the seemingly desperate woman?" Henry said.

"No of course not, I definitely do," James said with a smile.

"Okay we can follow her around but I don't want us to seem like we're stalking her, so try to be discreet about it," Jill said as they started slowly following around the woman with the panda bear. The fact that she had a giant stuffed panda bear made her stand out in the crowd so it was fairly easy to follow her.

After they had followed her for a while they could notice that every couple of minutes she seemed to be stopping and crossing her legs and bending at the knees a little bit.

"Do you think that maybe she will have an accident?" James said.

"Well I sure hope so," Henry said as he licked his lips.

Again Jill had to admit that she felt a little bit uncomfortable with the guys displaying so much animal lust towards this innocent woman with a very full bladder. At the same time though Jill had to admit that she was just as enamored with this woman and her current plight as they were. Having been desperate many times herself Jill could fully relate to what the woman was going through and that is why she felt a little bit bad about what they were doing. But she didn't want to play the hypocrite card; she enjoyed seeing other women having to pee just as much as these guys did, so she would be wrong to criticize them for it.

At the same time though she felt once again the guys don't understand what it's like to be a woman and to be desperate in the world, longing for a bathroom that you might not always find. But then Jill thought to herself that the woman should have taken that into consideration, so maybe she didn't deserve any sympathy.

As they continued watching the woman they could see that she was standing mostly still and seemingly jogging in place and it looked like she was using the panda to cover herself up holding the panda up in front of her.

"I think that she's probably going to have an accident," Henry said. "Look she is putting up her giant panda bear to hide any potential wet spots that appear on her clothing."

"I wish that my camera phone worked," James said as he took out his phone. "Oh wait, look it does actually work!"

"I think that videotaping this woman against her will might be going and crossing a line," Jill said as she continued staring at the woman who seemed to be holding her panda bear and looking quite frantic. "I have to admit I'm starting to feel bad for her."

"Why don't you go over to her and ask her if anything is the matter?" Henry said.

"Because I am socially awkward and approaching a woman that I don't know that I find attractive when she doesn't even know that I am a lesbian and that I am scoping her out because her bladder is about to explode, this makes the whole situation, I don't know, a little bit strange, don't you think?"

"Well screw it I think that I'm going to go over and see if she's okay," James said as he began walking over towards her.

"I guess we should follow him," Henry said as he and Jill reluctantly followed James over to the woman.

"Excuse me ma'am but you seem like you are lost or something," James said. "Is there any way I could be of assistance?"

The woman bobbed up and down holding her panda bear closely.

"Are you okay?" Jill asked.

"I feel really awkward admitting this but I really need a bathroom," the woman said. "Do you guys know where there might be a bathroom around here?"

Henry had to suppress the urge to smirk as he shook his head and smiled. "As far as we can tell this event didn't really have the foresight to think, hey maybe people are going to need the bathroom at some point."

"I bet that it was probably a bunch of old men who planned an event like this," Jill said. "You would think that from a business perspective if you provided bathrooms it would keep people around longer, once again especially seeing as the type of food and drink that they serve here tends to make one need to go."

"Well I don't live that far away so I guess I will just go home and go to the bathroom there," the woman said. "But thanks for offering to help."

"Any time," Jill said. "We ladies have got to stick together."

"So what does everyone want to do now?" James asked. "Do you see any more desperate women around Jill?"

"Nothing obvious," Jill said. "Like I told you most women try not to announce to the world in big bold flashing letters or in a big neon sign above their head that they have to go to the bathroom."

"Well I think that we should get something to eat, I didn't really eat earlier figuring that we were going to be at an event that serves food, so if anyone else wants to join me I think I'm going to go get something to eat," Henry said.

"It's your funeral," Jill said shaking her head. "I certainly wouldn't want to eat anything here."

They went over to the area where they were selling food and

Henry got some type of really big taco combination as did James. They both started scarfing it down at prodigious speed.

"Are you sure there isn't anything that you want to get Jill?" Henry asked as he finished up his taco. "The food here really isn't as bad as it seems."

Jill shrugged her shoulders. "I guess I could have a hot dog and some potato chips but then I'm going to need to get something to drink to go with that."

Jill reluctantly sat down and decided to have a hot dog with mustard and some potato chips and then she also got a really large soda that she drank rather quickly. She knew that it wasn't wise especially because she was already noticing a growing feeling of fullness in her bladder, and there was no way she wanted to run home to go to the bathroom before this event was over and let the guys know what was going to happen.

"Hey Jill do you think that maybe that woman might be desperate," Henry said as she saw a woman at the ring toss who seemed to be pacing in place.

Jill looked over at the woman and saw that she seemed to be jogging in place and looking around like she was searching for something.

"You know Henry I think that maybe you are starting to get better at this," Jill said. "I do think that something might be seriously wrong with that woman."

This woman was the first sighting that they had had of anyone who was very visibly desperate in the hour since they had eaten and drank something. But my now Jill had to admit that she was starting to think that maybe it was time to be heading home because she could feel that pressure in her bladder growing ever stronger by the minute.

"You think we should go over and talk to her?" James asked as he suddenly grabbed his stomach.

"Are you okay?" Jill said as she felt a rumbling in her own stomach. Did she have to do more than just pee? She certainly didn't want to contemplate the grim possibility of that.

"I think that I just have a little bit of indigestion or acid reflux," James said. "I think that I will try something when I get home, take some antacids or something."

"I have to admit I'm not feeling so hot myself," Henry said as he grabbed his own stomach. "In fact I am feeling really lousy all of the sudden, like I am burning up or something like that."

"Yeah I think I feel something like that as well," James said as he held his stomach.

"Maybe we should all just get going and get home," Jill said shaking her head. "I don't think that we're going to see any more desperate women today and I think that you guys are probably feeling the effects of eating tacos from a County fair that once again isn't smart enough to provide bathrooms."

"You're right, it doesn't really make business sense what they are doing," Henry said. "Just the same I think maybe I should call it a night and start getting home."

"So I guess I will see you guys later then," Jill said eager to make a mad dash to run home to use the toilet at home.

"See you later Jill," Henry said as he and James waved to her and watch her scampering off in the distance.

"You think that Jill is running home because she has to pee?" James said.

"Oh I don't doubt it for a second," Henry said as he and James slapped each other five before grabbing their stomachs and running back home to their own places.

As soon as Jill got home she ran into the bathroom, jerked down her skirt and sat on the toilet and had a really loud hissing pee.

Jill shook her head and smiled to herself. "You've still got it Jill, they didn't suspect a thing!"

Little did she know how much that was going to be changing in the near future.

3

Henry got home late that evening from the fair and had to admit that he wasn't really feeling that well. He decided that he would call it an early night and that maybe he could sleep off the fact that he was feeling indigestion and suddenly a bit feverish.

"Maybe Jill was right, maybe I shouldn't have eaten stuff at the town fair," Henry said as he felt his forehead. He put a thermometer in and realized that he had a temperature of 101°. "Oh great I probably have food poisoning now. But hopefully it will go away by morning time."

Henry sat in his bed feverish and he couldn't help but notice that suddenly he started seeing lots of colors that he hadn't remembered seeing before. His vision became blurry and everything began to sway. He thought that he saw a baby crawling around on the ceiling but maybe that was just because the day before he had watched the movie Trainspotting and it was influencing his hallucination.

The next morning he woke up and was feeling better and looked at himself in the mirror. He looked a little bit pale but he had gotten through the night without getting any sicker. He was starting to feel strange at the moment, like something was different, but he couldn't quite place his finger on what.

"Perhaps I should go for a walk or something," Henry said as he started walking around town. At first nothing seemed to be all that strange but then he started to notice something. He was checking out some attractive looking women and he couldn't help but notice that there seemed to be sort of a glow around them. He rubbed his eyes and shook his head but the glow was still there.

He decided that it was probably nothing and then maybe he was just feeling some effects of his fever still. He was hoping that nothing was wrong with his vision or anything like that but he couldn't help but notice that each woman that he saw was glowing a different color and level of intensity. Some of the women were glowing yellow, a couple blue, some green, a few of them orange and one woman he could see was glowing a bright red color and appeared like she was not feeling very well, and then she started running off like she had some place to get in a hurry.

"Oh great it seems like whatever I ate at that carnival yesterday has really screwed up my vision," Henry said shaking his head. "Well maybe it's temporary, whatever it is I hope that it goes away because this could be rather annoying." But he couldn't help wonder why some of the women were glowing different colors and different intensities of color than each other.

"Well I guess you really can't put too much thought into a hallucination, I'm sure it doesn't mean anything," Henry said as he continued jogging up and down the streets. But as he continued looking around he noticed something very distinctive. "I only see the glowing around women," he said as he looked up and down the street and continued rubbing his eyes. Whenever he looked at another man he didn't see any type of glowing around them.

"Okay now this is getting crazy, every time I look at a woman it's like a display of rainbow colors," Henry said as he continued walking up and down the streets. No matter how many women he looked at he couldn't help but notice that each one had their own distinctive color and intensity of glowing. He figured that the different colors probably meant something but he couldn't place his finger on what.

Henry ultimately decided as it was not going away and maybe he had better get his vision checked out, so he decided that he would go to the walk-in clinic and see if there was anything wrong with his eyes. If there was something going wrong with his vision he wanted to catch it now before it turned into something that was going to cause him problems later on.

As Henry was sitting in the doctor's office waiting to be called he couldn't help but notice that once again the women who were waiting in the office with him were all displaying their own distinctive glow.

However as he continued looking around he started to notice something curious. He saw that one woman was glowing a bright orange color and he couldn't help but notice she also seemed to be crossing and uncrossing her legs. Finally the woman got up and went to the desk.

"Do you have a bathroom around here?" the woman asked, looking nervous. The woman at the reception desk, who was glowing green, pointed her in the direction of the restroom which she ran into rather quickly.

Henry continued looking around the room and he noticed that a woman with a big belly who seemed to be pregnant was also looking rather uncomfortable and he couldn't help but notice that she was glowing a very bright red, a virtual explosion of colors.

He followed the pregnant woman with his eyes as she got up and waddled over to the bathroom and waited outside of the bathroom door. When the other woman emerged from the bathroom he couldn't help but notice that there was only a dim light glowing around her, almost barely perceptible. That was the first time he noticed the color of any woman that he had observed suddenly change. She had been orange but now she was barely a flicker of whiteness.

"Henry," the receptionist said as she waved him forward. As

the receptionist led him back to one of the waiting rooms for the doctor he couldn't help but notice that her green light had grown in intensity, as though it were becoming brighter and more obvious by the moment.

As Henry sat there waiting for the doctor to come and see him he looked around the room and he found that he didn't see the glow around anything else. He saw an image of female anatomy up on the wall showing an image of a woman with her skin transparent showing the location of all different organs. There was no particular glow around that woman, so it looked like whatever he was seeing only applied to living women and not just images of women in general.

"Can you give me a minute," Henry heard a female voice say.

"You have patients waiting," the voice of a man said.

A moment later the door opened and standing there was a rather attractive Asian woman who he couldn't help but notice seemed like she was a bit agitated. He also noticed that she was glowing a very bright and intense red. He had only seen one or two other women glowing that bright like this woman.

"Hi I'm Dr. Chung," the woman said as Henry couldn't help but notice that she seemed to be crossing her legs and bobbing up and down a little bit. "What seems to be the problem today?"

Henry felt weird telling this woman about his strange new condition but he decided that he had better tell her the truth because he wanted to get to the bottom of this and he didn't want anything to be wrong with his vision.

"I have to admit Dr. Chung, it's a little bit strange," Henry said. "I feel a bit strange talking about it."

"Well I'm the doctor, that's what I'm here for," Dr. Chung said and he couldn't help but notice that as she started shifting around more the bright red light around her seemed to be growing in intensity.

"Well it all started last night. I was at this carnival with my friends and I think I ate some type of bad taco or something like that. After eating it I started feeling indigestion and then I went home and was feeling really sick and feverish and my temperature was 101°. I decided I would just go to bed and hope that in the morning everything would be better. Although I was feeling better in the morning I noticed some type of weird symptom. I have never heard of anything like this before so I hope that it doesn't sound too strange."

"Well I'm a doctor, I have seen lots of strange things," Dr. Chung said as she bent at the knees a little bit.

"Okay but this is probably going to sound really weird. When I woke up this morning I realized that there seemed to be something wrong with my vision."

"You mean like you are seeing something? Were you seeing spots or was your vision blurry in any way? Here let me look in your eyes." Dr. Chung took out one of those little lights the doctors had and started shining it in his eyes. "Well your eyes don't look like they are any different. What type of things are you seeing exactly?"

"Well again here is the strange thing; I seem to be seeing some type of a weird glow around people."

"A glow around people, what type of glowing do you see around people?"

"Well I am seeing all different colors. I am seeing various shades of white, yellow, blue, green, orange and red."

"It sounds like you are seeing an entire spectrum of colors. And you say that you are only seeing this around people?"

"Well not all people. Here's the strange thing, I only seem to be seeing the glow around women specifically, and every woman seems to have a different glow. Every woman I have seen today has been glowing a different color and at a different level of intensity."

"Am I glowing right now?"

Henry nodded. "Yes you are doctor."

"What color am I glowing?"

"You are glowing a really very intense red, like blindingly red almost. Around your body seems to be sort of like a dark bright red field surrounding you. In fact you are probably the brightest woman that I have seen so far today."

"I take that as a compliment," Dr. Chung said as she smiled for the first time but still looked decidedly uncomfortable as she sort of shifted the weight of her legs and was now very noticeably and embarrassingly desperate. In fact watching the fact that she seemed to be squirming around like crazy was making it difficult for him to concentrate on what she was saying.

"Well actually I saw another woman who was glowing

almost as intense as you were, it was this pregnant woman in the waiting room."

"Well they say that pregnant women sometimes look like they are glowing but I have never heard anything quite as literal as this."

"So you haven't heard of anything like this before doctor?"

"Honestly I can't recall ever hearing anything like this. Your symptoms sound oddly specific, you see the glowing only around women and it seems like every woman has a different glow. Let me examine you more thoroughly. Please step into the other room so that I can examine your eyes more carefully."

Henry followed Dr. Chung down the hallway into another room and he couldn't help but notice that she seemed to be walking rather awkwardly, and she was glowing brighter by the moment, but eventually they stumbled into the next room. She then did a series of standard ophthalmologic examinations where she made him read eye charts and look through lenses and other things like that. He had to admit he didn't mind staring at her though because he could tell that she was obviously incredibly desperate for the bathroom.

"So what is the problem doctor?" Henry said.

Dr. Chung shook her head. "Your eyes seem to be fine but let me put some eye drops in and we will give you the exams again."

As soon as Dr. Chung had administered the eye drops she started running from the room and he could hear her jogging down the hallway.

"Doctor can I see you for a moment," she heard the man from before say.

"Give me a minute I really need to use the bathroom!" Dr. Chung said as Henry heard the sound of the bathroom door opening. It was like music to his ears as it confirmed everything that he had suspected, Dr. Chung had to go to the bathroom, and she had to go to the bathroom something pretty bad.

Henry went back to the waiting room to wait for his eye drops to take effect. Now his vision was more blurry but as he looked around at the women around him he still could see the glow around each of them. It was more blurry now, but it was still there nonetheless. And just like before every woman had a different color and a different level of intensity to the glowing.

He turned his eyes and looked at the receptionist and he

couldn't help but notice that now she was a bright orange color. Once again her color had changed and she seemed to be glowing brighter by the moment. It was hard to see through his blurred vision but he could distinctly see that she was definitely getting brighter and darker as the time went on. The outline around her was a nice warm orange glow, and the look on her face seemed to indicate that she was looking rather agitated. He also couldn't help but notice that she kept looking at the clock. He saw her reach for a bottle of water but then she put it down and shook her head.

Did this woman have to go to the bathroom as well, Henry thought to himself as he shook his head? When the receptionist called him back again he noticed that the receptionist looked kind of shifty in her own legs as she led him back to the examination room.

"How are you feeling," Dr. Chung said as she came back into the room looking more relaxed and with a smile on her face. He also noticed that now Dr. Chung was now a dim white color, her glow barely noticeable.

"Your color changed," Henry said.

"Oh did it?" Dr. Chung said.

"Yes you were glowing a really bright red before but now you are just sort of a dim white light. I also noticed that the receptionist also changed color to a brighter orange color."

"So you notice that women seem to be changing color now?"

"Yes, it's just something I suddenly noticed. Before all the women were staying the same color but I have noticed that as I observe women over a longer stretch of time their colors start to change, both the specific color and the intensity of the glow that surrounds them."

Dr. Chung looked over her papers and shook her head. "Well let us see if the eye drops made any difference."

Henry did the eye test again now with his eye drops in but when the tests were done Dr. Chung looked at Henry's chart again and shook her head.

"So what exactly is wrong with me doc?" Henry asked.

Dr. Chung shook her head once again. "Honestly looking at the results of your tests your vision appears to be fine. There doesn't seem to be anything physically wrong with your eyes. But I do find it interesting that you said that the colors of the women change. Have you noticed anything specifically that seems to cause the women's colors to change?"

Henry thought long and hard for a moment and that was when he suddenly had a revelation. He noticed that the women's colors appeared to change based on how badly they had to go to the bathroom. Then he thought to himself that sounded crazy and completely irrational. Maybe it was just his own mind projecting onto that.

"Seeing as there is nothing physically wrong with you I have to consider the possibility that maybe this is all in your head," Dr. Chung said. "It's possible that you are having some type of hallucination based on what's going on in your brain. However that would require further tests. You aren't feeling any type of pain are you? You haven't been having any type of weird thoughts or feelings?"

Henry shook his head. "No doctor, in all honesty the only strange thing seems to be that women have a glow about them that seems to be changing based on, well who knows what?" Henry in fact knew exactly what was causing them to change but he didn't want to say it to her.

"Well I would recommend that maybe you see a psychiatrist or a psychologist and maybe get your head examined. All I can tell you is that there is nothing physically wrong with your eyes and your eyesight appears to be normal, well aside from this weird anomaly."

"Well thank you for your help doctor and I will think about perhaps seeing a specialist if the problem persists, but it doesn't seem like it's harming me in any way," Henry said suddenly smiling.

"You suddenly seem like you are happy at this new condition," Dr. Chung said shaking her head.

"I'm just happy because you said that there is nothing physically wrong with my eyes, so maybe if I go to sleep tonight it will just go away." Now he was really hoping that it wouldn't go away, now that he understood what the colors meant.

Dr. Chung nodded. "Okay but if this persists I would seriously consider getting your head examined."

"Thank you for all your help doctor," Henry said as he shook Dr. Chung's hand.

As he left the doctor's office and walked out into the street he looked at all of the women that he saw and smiled. "The darker the color and the brighter the light the more they have to pee!" he said to himself as he laughed. He looked all around and he saw a barrage of colors coming from all the women and that was when he saw what he was hoping to see, another woman who was glowing bright red.

He didn't want to seem strange but he decided to follow her and he eventually followed her into a local coffee shop. Then just as he suspected he saw her get in line for the bathroom. He noticed that there were several women in line in front of her and he noticed that all of the women seemed to be glowing red or orange with maybe one or two who seemed like they were glowing green.

"They are all in line for the bathroom and they are all glowing really brightly," Henry said as he smiled. He felt like he had gained some type of new extraordinary super human power. As he contemplated this so many amazing thoughts were going through his head.

Just when Henry thought that things couldn't possibly get better, that was when he saw someone walk in the door and he couldn't help but notice that she had a healthy orange glow around her that seemed to be slowly turning red.

"Henry, what are you doing here," Jill said surprised to see him. "I thought you didn't really like coffee."

At this point Henry could barely contain his excitement because he could see the Jill was glowing an intense orange and he knew exactly what that meant.

"I thought you didn't really like coffee very much either Jill," Henry said that he couldn't help but notice that most of the women in the coffee shop seemed to be glowing brighter as they continued drinking.

That was when Jill realized that she was caught and Henry could see that she was trying to save face. He also noticed that she had her legs pressed tightly together. It was very subtle but because he was on the lookout for it he noticed it.

"I came into the coffee shop because I saw you," Jill said. "I wanted to make sure that you are okay since you weren't really feeling very well last night."

"Actually I'm feeling fine, thanks for asking," Henry said. "In fact I am feeling pretty great."

Jill smiled and nodded. "I am glad to hear it." Jill started looking in the direction of the bathroom line and looked like she was frowning.

"Are you looking for something Jill?" Henry said knowing very well what she was looking for. He wanted to try and keep her there as long as possible.

"No I just thought I saw someone that I knew," Jill said shaking her head. Henry looked back at the bathroom line and he saw the woman in the front of the line who was glowing bright red now was once again glowing a dim white, as were most of the other women who were coming out of the bathroom.

"Well are you doing anything right now Jill," Henry said continuing to smile as he could see that Jill's orange light was growing more intense by the moment and beginning to turn shades of red.

"Actually you know I think that I have some place that I need to be really urgently," Jill said as she started looking around.

"Where do you need to be?" Henry said trying his best to stall her and seeing that she was eager to get the hell out of there.

"I just have some stuff I have to do, but hey I will talk to you later," Jill said as she was about to leave.

"Wait a second Jill," Henry said as he grabbed her arm.

"What is it," Jill said looking more frantic and agitated by the moment.

"Do you see anything strange about those women in that line over there," he said as he pointed over to the bathroom line. He was kind of wondering if Jill perhaps had a similar ability.

Jill looked over at them. "If you are asking whether they are desperate I would say that at least some of them seemed to be. Like I said if they are in line for the bathroom you know that it means they must have to go to some degree. Honestly I would think you would probably be getting better at spotting this."

"I think I am getting better at spotting desperation Jill," Henry said as he looked at Jill's legs sort of rubbing together, albeit very subtly as she bent at the knees a bit. "But say don't you want to maybe watch some of these girls and see if they get desperate? Just think about it, we are in a coffee shop where all of these women are just continuously drinking, filling their bladders, that liquid just building up, and the pressure in their bladders growing by the moment."

"You know I'd love to but I think I really better be going," Jill said as she started walking towards the door. "I'll catch you later."

"Okay have fun Jill," Henry said as he walked towards the door and watched Jill running down the street now a bright red light and he could see that she stopped to grab herself every couple of paces.

As Henry looked up at the sky he smiled and folded his hands in prayer. "I don't know if you exist, but if you do, whatever this is, whatever gift that I have been given, please don't take it away, please let it last forever!"

Henry finished his prayer and began walking down the streets with a smile on his face and a spring in his step as he began to laugh evilly, maniacally even. "Time to go hunting for reds, and I ain't talking about Communists!"

In case this was temporary he was going to enjoy this day to maximum capacity as to waste an opportunity like this would be an affront to the bladder God!

4

Henry spent the rest of his day practically in a state of euphoria as he walked up and down the streets scouting them for women who were glowing orange and red. Occasionally he saw women of other colors as pretty much every woman had some degree of glowing around her, since almost everyone had to go to the bathroom a little bit unless they had just gone to the bathroom, but he was interested in the ones who were reaching the danger zone, so to speak.

That was when he saw it, another woman who was glowing bright red and he decided that he would approach her. He could see that she was looking around like she was searching for something.

"Excuse me miss I couldn't help but notice that you look like you are searching for something," Henry said as he approached her with a smile.

"No I'm fine, I'm not searching for anything," the woman said but Henry could see that she was clearly pressing her legs together and bending at the knee.

"Are you sure, you look like you are searching around for something, like you were deeply in need of something?"

The woman looked extremely awkward as she tried to control herself but Henry could see that her red glowing was getting out of control.

"Okay I won't lie," the woman said as she grabbed Henry by the arm. "I really need to use the bathroom but I can't seem to find any bathrooms available around here. All the stores say customers only or else the line has been just outrageous. If I don't find a bathroom soon I think I'm going to piss myself!"

It was total music to Henry's ears so he simply smiled and nodded. "I think I know where there is a bathroom around here," he said as he motioned her forward taking her in the opposite direction of where he knew the bathrooms were.

After a few minutes of wandering around seemingly aimlessly the woman looked like she was practically at the breaking point, and Henry had to admit that she was glowing so brightly he could barely see her.

"I'm going to freaking explode!" the woman said as she grabbed herself and danced in place. Now Henry was basically going completely crazy.

He tried his best to maintain his composure but this was like a dream come true. "Well I thought that the bathrooms were around here," he said shrugging his shoulders. "I guess I was wrong, maybe they got rid of them."

"I don't think I can hold it any longer," the woman said. "Do you think that you could stand guard for me?"

"Stand guard you say?" Henry said struggling to not get a powerful erection.

"Yeah I'm just going to go in the alley," the woman said as she looked both ways before going in the alley and pulling down her pants. Henry turned his back towards her but he tried to look out of the corner of his eye, and all he could notice was that as the woman slowly started hissing onto the sidewalk he could see that the glow from her was getting dimmer and going backwards through the spectrum of colors until he heard her pull up her pants and come out of the alleyway looking relieved.

"Feeling better?" Henry asked with a smile as he noticed that the woman was now glowing a dim white color indicating that her bladder was completely empty.

"Much better," the woman said smiling and shaking her head. "Thank you for being a gentleman and not looking and standing guard while I went to the bathroom."

"What kind of gentleman would I be if I didn't try to help a damsel in distress?" Henry said trying not to smirk too much.

"Hey I am no damsel in distress, but sometimes when you gotta go you gotta go."

Henry made small talk with the woman for a few more minutes but then she had to get on her way. He was tempted to follow her but he figured that now she was relieved and his interest had gone. Sure she was attractive but he probably didn't have a chance with her.

Henry continued wandering up and down the streets looking for more women who were "in the red" so to speak but the majority of them were the lighter colors of the rainbow indicating they didn't have to go very bad.

After a while Henry thought he saw a familiar face walking down the street.

"Hey James," Henry said walking over with a smile.

"Hey Henry, how are you?" James said coming over.

"I honestly couldn't be better!"

"I wish that I could say that, last night after we ate those tacos at the carnival, I felt so sick and everything, I went to sleep last night and I was all feverish and hallucinating and everything."

"So was I!"

"But it gets stranger than that, after that I started having all sorts of weird hallucinations and everything."

"Did you see the baby crawling on the ceiling as well?"

"What, no, what the hell are you talking about?"

"I guess you never saw the movie Trainspotting, you should, it's a pretty great movie, one of the best movies ever made about Scottish heroin addicts."

"How many movies have you seen about Scottish heroin addicts?"

"Well just Trainspotting and the sequel, but they were both pretty great movies."

"Well I didn't hallucinate about a baby on the ceiling okay. I am seeing all sorts of strange glowing colors and everything everywhere I go."

"But only around women?"

"What, yes, how on earth did you know that?"

"Because I have it too, everywhere you go you are seeing women who have a glowing around them and it changes colors and everything."

"Yes, that's it exactly, but again, how on earth did you know that?"

"I have it too, it must've been something that we ate, it must have been the crazy tacos or whatever."

"Well how the hell do we get rid of it?"

"Get rid of it, why on earth would you want to get rid of such a great miraculous gift from the heavens?"

"Well I think that there has to be something wrong, I mean if I start seeing this weird glowing whatever it is around women, well, don't you think that strange and alarming?"

"Dude, you totally have no idea what the glowing means do you?"

"Wait, it means something? This isn't making any sense."

"Let me show you. Come and walk with me and tell me what you see. What do you see over there?" Henry pointed to a woman who was looking relaxed and smiling.

"I see a woman, what about her?"

"What color is she?"

"She's yellow; she's glowing yellow, so what?"

"Well if she is glowing yellow she doesn't have to pee that bad."

"But if someone is really yellow doesn't that mean that they have to pee really badly?"

"No, the color codings have nothing to do with the color of urine. White is the lowest which means that they don't have to go at all, yellow means that they have to go a little bit, blue means that they have to go perhaps noticeably, green means that they probably can't ignore the urge, orange is desperate and red is a total emergency."

"How on earth did you figure out this whole system? Are you just bullshitting me?"

"No, I totally went to the optometrist and had my eyes examined because I thought I was going crazy or suffering a visual impairment, but as I started paying closer attention I noticed that the women of the darker color ranges had to go to the bathroom desperately and then after they went to the bathroom they became white again, meaning that they were empty."

"Get the hell out of here, seriously?"

"Well look at that woman over there, she's glowing red isn't she," Henry said as he pointed to a woman who looked like she was really agitated and bending at the knees a lot.

"That's right; she is glowing red, what of it?"

"Look at her bending at her knees constantly, she obviously has to pee really bad and the more she has to pee the brighter the red glowing is going to be. I'm telling you this new power allows us to know exactly when a woman is desperate and how desperate she is. I actually ran into Jill before and she was glowing red and then I saw her running off and grabbing herself."

"Holy shit dude, this is like a miracle, and this is like the greatest thing to ever happen in the history of the world. It still doesn't make any sense though."

"Who cares if it makes sense, as long as it doesn't go away I'm a pretty happy camper."

"But are you saying that Jill doesn't have the same ability?"

"I don't think so, I asked her if she saw anything unusual about some women waiting in a bathroom line and she thought that I was just asking if they were desperate, but she didn't say anything about seeing any glowing lights. So as far as I know we are the only people in the world who have this ability, and personally I think we should keep it secret."

"Even from Jill, I would think that she would want to know about something like this."

"Well of course she would stupid," Henry said as he bopped James on the back of the head. "But if she knows we have this ability we can't really use it to know when she is going to the bathroom. She will catch on to us and she will call us on our actions. If we keep this to ourselves we will always know when Jill has to go to the bathroom even if she isn't showing any obvious signs. Think of all the fun we can have with that, think of all the fun we can have with every single woman we meet! We now have a gift from the desperation gods; we know exactly how badly every woman on earth has to go to the bathroom and can see it gradually getting worse even if they aren't showing any other outward signs of it. I tell you this makes us gods, bladder gods."

"I have to admit it is pretty cool, maybe not as cool as having powers over the weather like Storm from the X-Men or Magneto from the X-Men using his magnetism powers, but it still a pretty cool ability."

"Screw the X-Men, they have lots of cool powers but this is like the power that is best suited for people like us. Sure it's not going to make us superheroes, and in some sense people might think that we would use this for villainous and evil ends, but hey you gotta take what the world gives you!"

"Well again it's pretty cool but I am still kind of wondering if there is going to be some type of long-term ramifications or long-term health effects of this startling new ability. What if tomorrow we wake up blind or our eyes fall out or something like that?"

"Dude you have to think positive. Sure perhaps anything can happen but we have no reason to think that anything is going to happen. I mean this is almost like we gained x-ray vision or something."

"X-ray vision would have been even cooler, because then we could see women naked!"

"That's true, but we can see something even better, we can know when any woman has to go to the bathroom and she can't hide it from us, that's better than x-ray vision any day."

"I suppose you are right, but I would still like to know where this power came from and how long it's going to last. Maybe we should seek out some expert advice."

"Yeah but if we told someone that we have this ability they would think we were crazy. I mean what if we tell the scientists we could see someone desperate to pee; they would think that we were kind of weird and creepy."

"Well aren't we?"

"Well yeah, which is all the more reason we should keep this secret to ourselves and just count our blessings."

"Well if science can't explain it maybe there is some type of other explanation."

"Are you actually suggesting that we should go to a church and ask a priest if we are being demonically possessed or something just because we have a perverted new power?"

"No I think we should go to the psychic over here," he said as he pointed to a sign in front of them that said psychic readings.

"Whatever."

The two of them shrugged their shoulders and went inside of the psychic where they saw what looked like a woman dressed like a hippie sitting in front of a crystal ball.

"You have come seeking answers from Mme. Melinda," the woman said as she waved her hands over the crystal ball.

James and Henry looked at each other and they both looked at Melinda who was glowing a fairly bright red color.

"Wow you really are psychic," James said. "We were kind of wondering, is it possible to suddenly gain weird new psychic abilities just out of the blue like that?"

"Have you had a near-death experience," Melinda said.

"I wouldn't say it was something as dramatic as that but we had some really weird tacos last night and now we seem to be seeing some type of glowing around women," Henry said.

"I think you have gained the ability to see auras," Melinda said. "An aura is a glow around a person that indicates their mental, physical and emotional state. It's like a window to their soul and perhaps even a window into the world beyond and their spiritual status."

"Yeah but ours is different, when we see auras it tells us when women have to pee," James said. "Have you ever heard anything like that?"

"What did you just say?" Melinda said as she raised her eyebrow. "Are you joking with me or something like that?"

Henry shook his head. "I assure you we are not lying to you. Can you see our auras?"

"Why do you have to go to the bathroom?" Melinda asked looking dismissive of what they were saying.

"No, but I know you have to go something pretty bad," James said with an evil smirk.

"Did my aura tell you that?" Melinda said as she crossed her legs.

"Yes it did," Henry said. "You are glowing bright red which means your bladder is about to explode."

"You guys are weird," Melinda said as she tapped her foot rapidly and seemed to shift around in her seat. Melinda was in fact going out of her mind desperate to pee.

"I don't know, you look awfully uncomfortable," James said as he smirked at Henry who nodded in agreement.

"You are weird guys, I don't have to go to the bathroom," Melinda said as she seemed to be staring angrily at the bathroom door across the room.

"Then you won't mind giving us a psychic reading, maybe a really long detailed one, a half hour type of reading," Henry said.

"You know that would be rather pricey," Melinda said as she crossed and uncrossed her legs as discreetly as possible underneath the table.

"Why, are you going anywhere?" James said. "I think I could use a really detailed psychic reading as well."

"Well it looks like you have about an hour of psychic readings ahead of you," Henry said.

"Do you think maybe you can give me a minute," Melinda said. "I think that I need to make a phone call."

"That's okay, we will wait for you to make a phone call over here," Henry said as he stood by the bathroom door. "Of course we can't wait forever; I mean if you don't want to give us our psychic readings now maybe we will take our business elsewhere."

Melinda gritted her teeth as she continued to squirm in her seat. "Fine," she said. "But let's make this quick as I have a very busy schedule," she said shaking her head.

"Not from what we saw outside," James said as he elbowed Henry.

"Let me go first," Henry said as he sat down across from Melinda and he couldn't help but notice that the table was shaking a little bit.

"What do you want to know?" Melinda said as she tried to maintain her composure. Henry knew that she was glowing so bright red that she could barely contain herself and this was driving him completely wild.

"I want to know the future," Henry said. "Read my fortune. So why don't you look into your crystal ball and tell me what the future holds?"

"What the future holds," Melinda said emphasizing the word holds as she reached into her table and took out some cards. "These are Tarot cards, please shuffle the deck and pick one."

Henry did as she said as slowly as possible as he continued watching her glow brighter and brighter and looking more and more frantic.

"I see a woman in your future," Melinda said as she looked at the cards.

"What type of a woman?" Henry asked.

"She seems like a friend," Melinda said. "And there's something about water?"

"Well hey I think we all like water sports," James said. "Who doesn't love to see all that water gushing around, just pitter pattering, trickling, hissing, gurgling."

"I'll be back in a minute," Melinda said as she got up and running towards the bathroom and slammed the door behind her.

Henry and James burst out laughing as they walked out of the psychic reading place and smiled.

"Well my friend I still have no idea how on earth we got this power, what it is or how long it's going to last, but I say we enjoy it while we can," Henry said. "Now the world is our oyster."

"And every single woman is our bitch!" James said as they both began laughing maniacally.

It was going to be a very fun day and they were both looking forward to it.

5

Henry and James were practically giddy after spending the entire day walking around town and finding where women had to go to the bathroom. They could never remember the last time that they had been so happy but everything seemed to be turning up really well for them, and they were looking forward to the next time that they would end up seeing Jill just so that they could demonstrate their fantastic power on her.

Jill got up the next morning to meet Henry and James at the bus stop because that was the day they were taking a bus trip into the city that they had all been looking forward to for a long time.

"Hi guys," Jill said as she approached Henry and James who were standing there smirking at each other. "You guys look awfully happy today."

"Why, should we look sad or something?" Henry asked.

"No of course not, I didn't imply that you should be sad," Jill said shaking her head. "There's just something about you guys, like you have some type of secret or something that you're not sharing with me."

"Why Jill, whatever could we be keeping from you?" James said trying not to look too obviously with a smirk at Henry.

"I don't know but you guys look like you are planning something, I know that look in your eyes, you guys are scheming up something aren't you?"

"We're just happy that we're going to probably see a lot of desperate women in the city," Henry said. "You're always telling us about how the city is always so crowded and how few bathrooms there are."

"Yes, we probably will see lots of desperate women in the city, but I don't intend to be one of them," Jill said shaking her head. "It's hard to find a bathroom in the city sometimes but I certainly don't intend to let myself get stuck in a situation where I am going to be desperate for the bathroom. I am always on the lookout for bathrooms; you know I have basically an eagle eye when it comes to finding bathrooms."

"Are you sure you don't have to pee Jill?" Henry said trying to hide his smirk.

"No I went to the bathroom not long before leaving," Jill said shaking her head. "I think by now you should know I always use the bathroom before leaving a place just as a precaution, that's something you have to do when you are a woman."

James shook his head. "Jill's right, I can tell just by looking at her that she is mellow yellow," he said as he couldn't help laughing as Henry joined in.

"What is so funny?" Jill asked with a light yellow glow surrounding her body.

"Nothing, it's just the way he said that I suppose," Henry said as he tried to suppress laughter once again.

"Are you guys laughing at something that I am not in on?" Jill said shaking her head.

"Okay we will be honest, it was kind of an inside joke, you'd have to be there to understand it so we really can't explain it to you," James said as he and Henry smiled at each other. They both knew that as she was only glowing yellow that Jill probably wouldn't have to go to the bathroom for a good while yet but the day was just beginning.

"Are you sure you don't have to go to the bathroom Jill?" Henry asked.

"No I'm good," Jill said with a smile and smirk as she stood there glowing bright yellow in front of the two guys. "In fact you may say I am mellow yellow."

The two guys looked at each other and began to burst out laughing again.

"I still don't see what's so funny about that, but I guess it is just a joke that I have to accept that I'm not going to understand," Jill said. "But look here comes the bus so let's get on quickly because we don't want it to leave without us."

The three of them paid their bus fare and as Henry and James looked for a place to sit naturally they were looking for a place that was glowing among the darker ranges of the colors. For the most part it looked like the bus didn't have that many women who were yet desperate to pee.

However as they continued walking down the aisles of the bus they saw that somewhere towards the back of the bus there seemed to be a woman who was glowing rather bright orange.

"Let's sit over here," Henry said as he directed them to a seat behind the woman who was glowing orange.

"Why do you want to sit all the way in the back of the bus," Jill said as she sat down between the two of them. "There were plenty of seats in the front of the bus."

"I think this is a pretty good seat Jill, like a front row seat to any of the action that might be happening in the bus," James said as he sat down next to her. "You probably just want to sit up front because you want to be the first one off of the bus so that you can get to the bathrooms right away."

Jill had to admit that they knew her routine pretty well but she didn't want to admit it to them while she was there, so she simply shrugged her shoulders and started to get comfortable. "I still don't think there's all that much to be seen on a bus," Jill said wondering why they seemed so insistent on sitting where they did.

Henry and James couldn't help but notice that the woman in front of them looked like her ears went up when they mentioned going to the bathroom.

As Jill put on her earplugs in order to listen to some music Henry and James began texting each other about the woman in front of them and how obviously she needed to go to the bathroom. Every so often they would look at Jill between them and realized that although she was still yellow little wisps of blue were starting to appear in her aura. They couldn't help but notice that as she drank from her bottle of water that her aura started to glow slightly more brightly by the minute.

The woman in front of them meanwhile was starting to become a very bright orange shifting into the red of the spectrum which got both Henry and James really excited. Finally Jill took out her earplugs when she was done listening to her music and she couldn't help but notice that the guys seemed to be texting away.

"Are you guys sending each other messages?" Jill asked. "I hope you're not talking about me."

Henry sent Jill a text message that said I think the woman in front of us has to go to the bathroom really bad but I didn't want to say anything.

What makes you think that, she isn't showing any really obvious signs, Jill texted back?

Men's intuition, Henry texted back.

Is that even a thing, Jill replied?

Sure if women can have intuition why can't men, Henry texted.

As Jill began texting with Henry she did look ahead of her and couldn't help but notice that the woman in front of her seemed to be shifting around a little bit in her seat, and Jill could hear that she was tapping her shoes really loudly on the bus floor in front of them.

10 to 1 odds that woman has to pee, James texted the both of them.

I think you are right, Jill texted.

She's far beyond the stage of mellow yellow, Henry said with lots of smiling emoticons as James and Henry began snickering.

"I am still not getting the joke," Jill said aloud as the woman in front of her grew louder with her feet tapping.

"Excuse me driver!" the woman front of them said as she waved her hands.

"What is it?" the driver asked over the intercom.

"It is really embarrassing for me to have to ask but I thought that this bus was going to have bathrooms and I guess I didn't plan accordingly when I found out that it didn't," the woman said.

"I'm sorry but we are stuck in traffic so you will just have to wait until we arrive at our destination," the driver said.

"Dammit," the woman cursed under her breath.

"Sounds like a red alert," Henry said as he looked at James

because now the woman was glowing a very bright red.

"Yeah I think that she really has to go," Jill said trying not to speak to loudly.

"Hey you might be at red alert stage soon though," James said.

"I think that Jill right now is green with envy," Henry said as he smirked at James because now they could see the Jill was starting to glow a green color.

"What am I green with envy over?" Jill said as she shook her head. Maybe they thought she was green with envy because the woman had to pee but why would Jill envy something like that?

"It's another inside joke Jill, you are just going to have to accept that not all jokes can be understood by everyone," Henry said.

"Mellow yellow, red alert, green with envy, is it just me or are you saying a lot of color related jokes today," Jill said suddenly catching on.

"It's probably just you Jill," James said as he and Henry continued to look straight forward seeing that the woman was now a very bright red and it didn't look like there was that much longer for her to go before the grand finale exploded.

"Hey orange alert," James said as he looked at the woman sitting next to the woman in front of them.

"Are you talking about orange, what is this like some type of terrorist system or something?" Jill asked. "Like they have raised the terror alert to orange or something, I'm starting to be getting sick of all your color coding jokes, I would really like to be in on this."

"I already told you Jill it's an inside joke, if you weren't there you wouldn't get it," Henry said.

"I don't know maybe I would get it if you just explained it to me," Jill said.

"It's kind of a guy thing," James said. "Don't take it personally, we're not excluding you based on gender, it is just it's humor a woman wouldn't get."

"Why is it something perverted?" Jill asked. "I think that you know that women can be just as big pervs as you guys, well okay maybe not as big as you guys specifically, but guys in general."

By now the three of them were all focused on the fact that the woman in front of them was now tapping her feet so loudly probably no one could ignore it.

"Dammit I really have to go," the woman in front of them cursed under her breath.

"I kind of have to go pretty badly too," the woman next to her said.

"God it must be embarrassing that the whole bus knows they have to go to the bathroom now," Jill said. "There's nothing more embarrassing than when guys know you have to pee."

"Do you need to pee Jill?" James asked with a smile.

"No I'm still good," Jill said as she drank from her water bottle before looking at her watch and frowning.

"I don't think that she is at orange alert yet," Henry said.

"Again with the color coding," Jill said. "Wait, does the color coding have something to do with pee?"

James looked at Henry quick before looking at Jill. "Why would you think that Jill?" James asked.

"Okay Jill I'll level with you, it's kind of a military thing, codes and stuff like that," Henry said.

"And what because I'm a woman you don't think that I can understand military codes," Jill said. "That's kind of sexist."

"Again it's more complicated than just military codes, you really had to be there," James said shaking his head.

"Okay I seriously need to go to the bathroom now," the woman in front of them said as she waved her hand at the bus driver.

"I'm sorry lady but we're stuck in traffic," the bus driver said.

The woman was going to continue arguing but as Henry and James saw her light go from red to orange to green and then rapidly down to white they just suddenly realized that she had peed herself.

"Gross you had an accident," her friend said next to her as she started tapping her feet loudly because now she was at stage red as well.

"I'm impressed, you guys have gotten more attuned to when women have to go to the bathroom," Jill said. "Even I didn't pick up at that woman was desperate until she said something. How on earth did you know that?"

"Like I said, men's intuition," Henry said. "Believe me it's a thing."

"Is there anyone else you think on this bus is desperate," Jill said as she looked around not seeing any obvious signs of desperation, but then again most women were seated and all she could see was the back of their heads.

"Oh I think a lot of people in this bus are in the red zone," Henry said.

"I bet you have to pee a little bit don't you Jill," James said. "Maybe not an emergency yet but I'm guessing you probably have to go at least somewhat don't you?"

"Well that's just none of your business, a lady doesn't tell about those things," Jill said unable to deny that she was feeling a noticeable urge to go to the bathroom now. She wasn't yet at the desperate stage but she very distinctly had to go and she couldn't help but start looking at her watch again.

"I would say most people on this bus don't have to go to the bathroom too badly right now but there are definitely a lot of people in the red zone and a couple of people under orange alert," James said.

"I really wish you would stop with all the color-coded military talk," Jill said. "I feel like I am being left out of something really big here."

"It's nothing special Jill, like I told you it's a guy thing, you had to be there," Henry said. "But if I had to bet I would say that the woman in the front of the bus is probably the next one who's going to have to go to the bathroom."

"Well unless she says anything there's no way to know who won the bet," Jill said.

"Okay everybody we're finally here," the driver said as the bus came to a stop.

"Finally!" the woman in the front of the bus said as she bolted off of the bus.

"There she goes, they're off!" Henry said.

As everyone piled off of the bus Henry and James couldn't help but smile and smirk as they saw the reds and the oranges rapidly run to the front of the bus and get out of there. Those glowing the lighter colors they noticed were going more leisurely.

As the three of them walked off the bus and into the warm summer weather Jill couldn't help but notice that Henry and James seemed to be having that thousand yard stare but she had no idea what exactly they were looking for.

"I guess it's a guy thing," Jill said as she shrugged her shoulders and the three of them began to walk.

6

As the three of them walked down the city streets Henry and James could both see that Jill was picking up the pace as she started glowing a healthy green. As they passed by the park Jill started to blend in with all of the green trees and everything around her.

"Wait up Jill, we almost lost you," James said as Jill paused to allow them to catch up to her.

"Yeah you practically blend in with all of these trees," Henry said as he caught his breath.

"How do I blend in with all the trees, I am not wearing anything green?" Jill asked still perplexed.

"I guess you just have sort of a green glow about you," James said as Henry covered his mouth.

"James can I talk to you alone for a moment," Henry said as he pulled James over to the side out of the listening distance of Jill.

"Is something the matter?" James asked.

"Look if we want to keep this secret between us I think that maybe we should stop talking about all of the color coding," Henry said. "I think that Jill is starting to catch on to us."

"You think that she knows that we know that she has to go to the bathroom?"

"I don't know, but I do know that Jill is getting a darker green so in a short amount of time she's going to have to go to the bathroom pretty badly. So I think that our strategy for the day should be to try and not let Jill out of our sights for a minute. If we leave her alone she will find the opportunity to go to the bathroom and we don't want that. We want to see her have to admit that she is desperate to go to the bathroom."

"I don't know she can be pretty stubborn about not letting people know that she wants to go to the bathroom."

"Yeah but we also know that she can only hold out so long and she is not going to risk having an accident. As soon as she reaches the emergency level she will have to cave and use the bathroom and we will get a nice little show."

"Sometimes I feel guilty about potentially embarrassing her like this, but on the other hand it's really fun to hear a woman acknowledge the fact that she has to go to the bathroom really bad and then tease her about it."

"We shouldn't feel too guilty; we know that Jill enjoys desperation as well, although we should definitely keep our newfound power secret because it would make her as jealous as hell."

"I wonder why Jill didn't get weird new psychic powers as well."

"Well that's obvious; she didn't eat those disgusting tacos that made us sick. Whatever was in those tacos for some reason gave us the psychic power to read auras, but only in regards to women having to go to the bathroom."

"I guess we really are blessed. I mean that is such an oddly specific affect from food poisoning and such an oddly specific thing that it would allow us to do, and of all people to know when women have to pee, honestly what are the odds?"

"Like I said, don't look a gift horse in the mouth. We have to milk this new ability for all it's worth."

"What are you guys talking about over here," said Jill, who was now glowing even brighter green. "You guys aren't conspiring against me or something are you?"

"Calm down girl, you are so damn suspicious," Henry said shaking his head. "We just had some guy stuff to talk about."

"You mean men's intuition?" Jill asked rolling her eyes in a dismissive manner.

"Yeah, something like that, it really is a thing," Henry said. "In fact it can be quite a wonderful thing."

"Well let's just hurry and get to the zoo quickly because the park doesn't even have –" Jill said before she stopped talking.

"Because the park doesn't have what?" James asked.

Jill realized that she almost gave herself away so she immediately changed gears. "Because there is absolutely nothing worth seeing in the park, at least at the zoo we will get to see all kinds of weird animals from around the world."

"Okay let's get going then," Henry said as he and James trailed slightly behind Jill trying not to go too fast. They didn't want to go too slow because then they thought Jill would get suspicious again. But if they just barely managed to keep pace with her they could delay her from getting to a bathroom for that much longer.

"I can see some wisps of orange appearing in her aura," James said with excitement.

"What did you say about orange?" Jill said as she stopped and turned around looking at them.

"I said do you want to get some orange juice," James said. "Walking around the city is hot thirsty work and I think that we should make an effort to stay well hydrated don't you think?"

"I'm good," Jill said as she took a sip from her water bottle. "Besides orange juice always makes me have to go to the bathroom more. But let's hurry; we are almost at the zoo."

Not long after that they arrived at the zoo but unfortunately there was a long line to get in, but Henry and James didn't seem to mind as they could see that Jill's green aura was gradually becoming a light orange color.

"Come on come on what is taking so long," Jill said as she tried to look at the front of the line and seemed to be looking more agitated.

"Are you in a hurry all of the sudden Jill?" Henry asked.

"I just don't like waiting around forever just to get into the zoo," Jill said shaking her head. "The sooner we get inside the sooner we can get to the –"

"Get to the what?" James asked.

"The sooner we can get in and start seeing all the animals," Jill said as her orange glow grew brighter.

Finally they got into the zoo and found themselves in the sea animals district.

"But where should we start?" James said. "I guess since we were in the water area we might as well take in the sights first."

"I don't know, why don't we, you know, just look around and see what we see," Jill said as she looked at the map and saw that the bathrooms were on the other side of the park.

"Hey it's no rush," Henry said shrugging his shoulder. "I say that we stay here and that we look at the sea life first."

"I second that notion!" James said. "It looks like it's two to one Jill."

"Okay but let's not spend too much time lingering here as we have an entire zoo that we want to see before the day is over," Jill said as she as subtly as possible crossed her legs.

"Look at all the water spouting from the blowholes of that dolphin," James said.

"Yeah that's really something," Jill said as she crossed and uncrossed her legs and put her hands into her pockets. "But hey I think we should keep moving, I really want to see the monkeys!"

"Hey why don't we take one of those the zip lines or whatever they are, you know where you can go over the whole park in like a trolley car or whatever," Henry said.

Jill looked at the map. "Actually that would be the quickest way to get to the ba –"

"To get to where Jill?" Henry asked.

"To get to the baboons, let's go see the baboons and their raw red asses," Jill said.

"Jill I never realized you were so into ass," James said. "I'm an ass man myself."

"Sure I love a nice ass, whether it be a nice shapely human ass or the ass of some type of filthy disgusting animal," Jill said as the three of them had a laugh and got in line to go zip lining across the park.

Finally as they were above the park Jill relaxed a little bit as she noticed that soon that they would be to the bathrooms as the bathrooms were right at the end of the zip lining. Henry and James couldn't help but notice that Jill was now tapping her fingers and tapping her feet a real lot even though she was trying not to show it.

"Red alert," Henry said as he elbowed James while looking at Jill.

"Red alert, what are you talking about?" Jill said.

"I'm just saying if you look out the window you can see the bird sanctuary," Henry said.

Jill very slowly looked around behind her and saw that indeed there were birds flying around and they were going right by. Henry and James meanwhile had their eyes directly trained on Jill who was now glowing a very obvious red and they were both smiling.

"What are you guys so happy about?" Jill asked, not even realizing that she had crossed her legs in a very obvious manner.

"Once again would you rather us be unhappy Jill?" Henry asked.

"It's nothing Jill, we are just having a really good time at the zoo here with you," James said.

That was when all the sudden they stopped halfway across the park.

"We are experiencing some slight delays and malfunctioning, just stay in your seats and everything will be fine," an announcement said.

"How long of a delay?" Jill said as she started to squirm around in her seat hardly able to disguise it.

"Is something the matter Jill, you seem distressed," James said.

"That's it guys, out with it," Jill said.

"Whatever are you talking about Jill?" Henry asked as he looked at James like he was confused.

Jill shook her head. "Don't play ignorant with me; don't think I haven't noticed that you guys have been acting strange lately, pretty much all day. I want to know what is up and I want to know what is up now."

"You probably wouldn't believe us if we told you Jill," Henry said.

"Probably wouldn't believe you if you told me what?" Jill asked.

"The fact that we have phenomenal psychic powers!" James said.

"Phenomenal psychic powers?" Jill said shaking her head. "No really, what is up with you guys?"

"Come on Jill we know you believe in all sorts of crazy paranormal stuff, why is it so hard to believe that we have amazing psychic powers," Henry said.

"Just out of the blue like that?" Jill said. "And what specific psychic powers do you have?"

"We know when people have to pee!" James said. "And not just that but how badly they have to pee as well."

"What the hell?" Jill said. "Are you guys seriously playing a joke on me?"

"Well it's not all people, it's just, well, it's just women," James said slightly blushing.

"Right," Jill said as she raised her eyebrow. "So you have this phenomenal psychic power and all it lets you do is know how badly women have to go to the bathroom? And you don't find that sort of an odd coincidence, that you guys of all people would have a power that specific so catering to your interest?"

Henry shrugged his shoulders. "What can I say, it's true Jill.

We were kind of wondering why you don't have the same powers as us."

"What type of powers?" Jill asked.

"The power to see how badly women have to go to the bathroom," James said. "It all happened after we ate those really weird tacos at the carnival that day. We figured that because you didn't eat the tacos you didn't gain this awesome new ability to know when women have to pee."

"Oh I know when women have to pee, I don't need psychic powers for that," Jill said as she was now shifting around a lot and could not hide it any longer.

"That's how we knew that the women on the bus had to pee, both of them," Henry said.

"And how exactly does this power work, how does it let you know how badly women have to go to the bathroom?" Jill said.

"Well it's kind of like reading auras, at least that's what that psychic lady told us before she had to run to the bathroom herself," James said.

"That was what all of our color talk was about," Henry said. "The fact is we see sort of like a glowing aura around women varying on the color spectrum where the darker the colors become the more women have to pee. Basically red is the worst and right now we can tell that you are glowing red. Be honest with us Jill, you can't even hide the fact that you have to go to the bathroom."

"Okay I think that you guys can probably tell it's obvious at this point that I really need the bathroom," Jill said as she squirmed around. "That's not enough to make me believe that you suddenly have gained phenomenal psychic powers, particularly something as ridiculous as the only ability that you have is the ability to tell how badly women have to go to the bathroom."

Finally they started moving again.

"Thank God!" Jill shouted as they rapidly approached their destination. She practically pushed the two of them in down to get out of the zip line and ran towards the bathroom only to see that there was a huge line of women. "Of all the times!"

"Hey what an awesome line," Henry said as he came over and saw Jill in line.

"Not awesome if you guys had to wait in it!" Jill said. "I'm ready to explode here!" By now she was uncontrollably crossing her legs and uncrossing them and dancing in place.

"Speaking of the bathroom I think that we could use a trip to the bathroom," James said as he and Henry went to the men's room, which of course had no line whatsoever.

"You gotta go don't you?" the girl in front of Jill said.

"Is it that obvious?" Jill asked with a smile. By then Henry and James had come back and were standing there watching Jill in line. She of course didn't want to say anything because she didn't want to out herself as a desperation watcher, but right now she was feeling rather awkward and somewhat angry at her two friends.

"You should let our friend cut," Henry said to the girl in front of Jill in line. "You don't really have to go to the bathroom that badly. Be honest, are you just waiting in line out of precaution because you think you're going to have to go later?"

"I guess it's not an emergency but how on earth would you know that," the girl said.

"You are just looking blue," Henry said.

"What do you mean I am looking blue, you think I am looking sad so that means you think that I don't really have to go to the bathroom that bad?" the girl asked.

"He means that your aura is blue," James said.

Jill knew exactly what the guys meant when they were talking about her aura but she didn't want to butt in and say that her friends thought that she had to go to the bathroom because they had some magical psychic abilities.

"All I am saying is that most of the women in this line are in blues and greens and maybe a couple of orange, I think that Jill you are the only one who is in a red alert," James said.

"What the hell your friends talking about?" the girl in front of Jill said shaking her head.

"It's probably some type of an inside joke again," Jill said as she looked at them angrily. "Isn't it guys?"

Henry and James smiled and nodded at each other as Jill waved away a bunch of bees that were flying around the garbage cans near the bathroom.

"I hate bees!" Jill said as she tried to escape from the bees.

"Well don't get out of line Jill, you don't want to lose your place!" James said as he began laughing.

"I bet you guys think this is a real laugh riot," Jill said as she danced up and down. "Well enjoy the show now because it's going to be over soon."

But nearly 25 minutes later Jill was just nearing the front of the bathroom. A few minutes later when it was finally her turn the girl in front of her went to the bathroom but she didn't sound like she had to go that bad. When Jill finally went to go she practically just made it and it was so satisfying and she came out looking a lot happier than before.

"Well I can see you feel better Jill, you are no longer in the red zone," James said. "But be honest did the woman in front of you have to go to the bathroom that bad?"

"Well I don't think she had an emergency if that is what you're talking about," Jill said shaking her head. "But it is going to take more than that to convince me that you have some type of psychic powers to see when women have to go to the bathroom."

But as the three of them walked away from the bathrooms to go over and see the red asses of the baboons the thought never left Jill's mind. When she looked at the red of the asses of the baboons she wasn't thinking of their asses, she was thinking of what they said about her being in the red zone and it sent a chill up her spine.

As they prepared to leave the zoo to go catch a train Jill couldn't help but shake her head and wonder to herself. "What if they are right?"

7

Jill noticed as she was leaving the zoo that Henry and James were having a good look up and down the line of women heading towards the bathroom.

"Using your phenomenal psychic powers?" Jill said as she came over to them shaking her head.

"Yes something like that," Henry said. "It really is pretty awesome, now we can always know when women have to go to the bathroom; it's like a dream come true."

"Which is exactly why I don't believe it," Jill said. "I mean I believe in psychic powers but the idea that you have a specific psychic power to know when women have to go to the bathroom and how badly just seems like it's really stretching credulity."

"Why not?" Henry said. "I mean if psychic power can tell you all sorts of different things such as remote viewing or seeing the future and all this other stuff, then why couldn't you have a psychic ability to know when women have to go to the bathroom?"

"I think he's got you there Jill," James said.

"I don't know, it's just that I've heard about lots of other psychic phenomenon but I have never heard of anyone specifically having a psychic ability to know how badly someone else has to go to the bathroom," Jill said shaking her head. "It just doesn't make a whole lot of sense."

"Maybe we are the first ones to have this specific psychic ability and nobody has noticed it before," Henry said. "We could be the next stage in human evolution. We will be a group of super powered mutants who have the ability to know conclusively which women have to go to the bathroom and how badly. It's almost like Darwin's theory of evolution, basically if it has some type of useful function it will be passed on to the next generation. It's an adaption, to a world of uncertainty, the terrible uncertainty that comes with not knowing when women have to go to the bathroom."

"Let's not get ahead of ourselves here," Jill said. "Even if theoretically speaking you did have this ability, and I am not saying that you do, I hardly think that it's the next stage of evolution or justified to consider yourself superhuman simply because you can tell when women have to go to the bathroom. I mean I don't have psychic powers but I can often look at a woman and tell if she has to go to the bathroom."

"I don't know Jill it sounds like you're just jealous that we have superpowers and you don't," James said.

"Well I'm not convinced that you have superpowers yet, but yes you can tell when women have to go to the bathroom simply by looking at them without even having to look at any signs or body motions, that's pretty freaking sweet!" Jill said as she shook her head. "You're damn right I would like an ability like that! So just out of curiosity, and again I'm not saying that I believe that you have this special power, but which of these women is your psychic power telling you has to go to the bathroom right now?"

James looked at Jill and shook his head. "Well you have to go to the bathroom, no denying that, but you aren't at the point where you are yet at an emergency. You're not quite desperate but I'm guessing that you are probably feeling uncomfortable and the way you are looking at that bathroom right now I'm thinking you are probably thinking, maybe I should go to the bathroom before I leave the zoo. Is that anywhere in the ballpark?"

Jill had to admit that he was completely 100% accurate. She wasn't yet at the emergency stage but she was definitely seriously thinking about going to the bathroom if not for the fact that the lines were so long, but she wasn't about to admit that to them.

"I'm not telling, that's a secret," Jill said. "Now is there anyone else aside from me in that line that you think has to go to the bathroom?"

"Red alert at 3 o'clock," Henry said as he pointed to a woman who wasn't even in line for the bathroom.

"But she's not in line," Jill said.

"Maybe not but she definitely has to go," Henry said. "I'd be willing to bet that she is going to get in line any second now."

"She's not even showing any obvious signs that she has to go," Jill said as the woman looked like she was standing very still and smiling.

The three of them continued looking at the woman who very slowly walked towards the end of the bathroom line and looked like she was frowning and suddenly looked very nervous.

"Told you so, believe me now?" Henry asked.

"It's a lucky guess," Jill said still not wanting to believe it. "Is there anyone else who seems like they have to go to the bathroom really bad?"

"Here comes a group of women, two greens, a blue, an orange and a red, I would be pretty shocked if that group didn't use the bathroom before they left," Henry said as he pointed at the group of women who just as he suspected got in line for the bathroom.

"Again it doesn't prove that you have psychic power," Jill said.

"I think that Jill is just green with envy," James said with a smirk. "Green with envy, green with envy, green with envy."

"You don't have to keep repeating yourself!" Jill shouted.

"What's the matter Jill, getting agitated, feeling some type of pressure," James said as he laughed.

"No you're just being very annoying and immature," Jill said as she looked at the very large line to the bathroom. She really did want to get in line and use the bathroom but she also didn't want to confirm the suspicions of these two guys because then they would never let her live it down.

"Well I think that we will use the bathroom before we leave," Henry said as he and James walked into the empty men's room causing Jill to bite her lip.

"You know sometimes I really hate those guys," Jill said as she shook her head and looked at the women's bathroom line and ran to the front of the line. "Excuse me I'm kind of in a rush to leave with my friends; do you think I could cut in line for the bathroom?"

"Absolutely not, this is an emergency here," the woman said as she pointed Jill towards the end of the line.

As Jill approached the end of the line she couldn't help but notice the woman that they pointed out who was really agitated and they said was a red alert. Jill was insanely curious but felt kind of awkward asking her. But she couldn't resist.

"Wow this is some line isn't it," Jill said as she looked ahead. "I just tried to cut in line but nobody would let me."

"Well we all have to go just as bad," the woman said with a harsh tone to her voice.

"You sound like you are in the emergency zone," Jill said.

"I can't remember the last time I had to pee this bad," the woman said shaking her head.

"Wow you hardly are even showing it though," Jill said shaking her head. "You must have pretty good self-control."

"Hey not everybody shows it when they have to go, but I certainly do have to go."

"I know I have these two guys with me and I just never want to admit when I have to go to the bathroom. I mean right now I kind of have to go to the bathroom, not as bad as you do, but I would sure like to use the bathroom before I leave, but I'm not about to wait in line for 20 minutes and delay them and have them standing there watching and laughing as I stand in line. So I will just wish you good luck in getting to a bathroom in time."

"Same to you," the woman said to Jill as she saw Henry and James coming out of the men's room. "But anyway they are my friends and I have to get going now."

As Jill walked over to Henry and James they had smiles on their faces.

"Hey you talked to the red alert woman," James said. "You were curious as to whether she had to go to the bathroom, weren't you?"

"Did she really have to go as bad as we thought?" Henry asked.

"Gentlemen I will say what the government always says when there is a UFO crash that they don't want to admit, I will neither confirm nor deny it," Jill said as she shook her head.

"She has to pee," Henry and James said as they looked at the woman.

"And your green is getting pretty bright Jill, maybe a few wisps of orange," Henry said. "But hey it's getting late so if we want to catch our train in time we can't wait around in this long bathroom line."

"You guys always just love to really rub it in whenever there is no line for you guys but a huge line at the ladies room," Jill said shaking her head.

"But of course Jill, because we know it annoys the living hell out of you," Henry said. "But nonetheless we really do have to get going if we want to catch our train in time."

The three of them started walking towards the train station. Jill felt relieved in some sense because at least at the train station they might have bathrooms. Although she wouldn't admit it to them she definitely was in the orange going by their standards, meaning that she wasn't quite in the emergency level but she was in the stage where she was getting quite desperate. The buses never have bathrooms but there were usually bathrooms at the train station. She just hoped that they would get there in time for her to use the bathroom.

"What a lovely sea of orange and red," Henry said as they arrived at the train station where Jill saw an ungodly long line at the ladies room, once again next to a nonexistent men's room line.

"And since I know you are probably going to ask Jill, no we don't have time to wait in that line if we are going to catch our train on time," James said as he patted her on the back. "Which really sucks for you because I can see that you are getting pretty orange."

"Shut up," Jill said. "I'll be fine." Jill had to grit her teeth because she knew that it would be at least an hour before they got home and she did not look forward to having to wait that long before she got to the bathroom again.

Jill followed Henry and James down to the train platform where she had to admit that now she was struggling not to be obvious about the fact that she was crossing her legs. She figured if she was as subtle as possible maybe it wouldn't be noticeable, but she knew that all eyes were on her so she would have to try harder to maintain her composure if she didn't want to give herself away.

"Well it looks like a lot of women down here didn't get to go to the bathroom either," James said. "So many oranges and reds and a whole bunch of blues and greens as well."

"Now you're just doing that to annoy me," Jill said as she stood up on her tip toes as subtly as possible to make it look like she was just looking for the train.

"Hey you can take our advice or not but I am just telling you that there are lots of women waiting for this train who really have to pee almost as bad as you, if not more," James said.

"Yeah like that woman," Henry said as he pointed to a woman standing very nonchalantly standing on the train platform and looking around.

"Are you sure, she doesn't look very desperate?" Jill said.

"Not to the untrained eye, but to those of us with extraordinary psychic power we can see things that most mere mortals can't," James said.

"I really doubt that you can tell if that woman has to go to the bathroom or not," Jill said shaking her head.

"You're just jealous because we can spot desperation better than you can now," Henry said. "We can spot the desperation when it's not obvious. Like right now we know that you have to pee like crazy and you are just trying your best not to admit it to us but we know that is just driving you completely and utterly mad."

"That's not true," Jill said knowing full well that was totally true and that all she could think about was getting to a bathroom.

"Then why haven't you been taking any sips from your water bottle lately," Henry said.

"I'm just not thirsty right now," Jill said as she licked her lips now not able to get the thought of drinking from her water bottle out of her head.

"Jill has to pee," Henry said as he began laughing.

"You guys are so immature," Jill said shaking her head as the three of them went and looked back at the nonchalant woman to realize that she was going off in the corner and appeared to be squatting down. "What is she doing?" But of course Jill knew full well what she was doing.

"Oh wow we are going to get a pee sighting!" Henry shouted. "I knew that that woman had to pee like crazy. I hate to say I told you so Jill, but I totally told you so!"

"This is the best power in the history of the world," James said. "Okay maybe not as cool as Storm or Magneto from the X-Men, but still pretty damn awesome."

The three of them couldn't help but stare at the woman as she went and seemingly peed for like a minute or two before she finally got up and nonchalantly walked back over to the train platform leaving a large visible puddle for all to see.

Jill had to admit it was a good sighting but at the same time she had to admit that she pretty much wanted to scream because she wished that she could do with that woman was able to do.

"I bet you wish that you could have popped a squat as well," Henry said.

Did they have mind-reading powers now? Jill thought to herself. No, now you're getting paranoid Jill, she told herself, but she found herself believing it more and more by the moment that maybe there was something to what they were saying after all.

Jill wanted to say something to break the awkward silence and she thought that Henry and James were about to say something when all the sudden she saw the train coming. "Hey it's the train!" Jill shouted as she pointed at the oncoming train glad to finally have something other to talk about aside from extremely full bladders, of which hers was definitely one.

The three of them piled onto the train to see that it was jam-packed since it was rush-hour. There wasn't a single place to sit down which disappointed Jill greatly because it was always harder to hold a full bladder when you had to stand up.

"Damn it looks like it's packed," Henry said suddenly smirking. "But luckily a lot of these people have to go to the bathroom, just like you do Jill." Henry elbowed Jill in the side which she had to admit almost caused her to lose her balance and that jostled her bladder a little bit.

"Okay I'll bite, who on this train happens to be desperate?" Jill said.

"See that woman at the other end of the train car," Henry said as he pointed to an attractive pale skinned woman with really long black hair.

"Yeah she's not bad looking," Jill said as she started looking at the woman very carefully and noticed a slight twitching of the leg. "And I think that she actually is showing signs of desperation."

"So you believe me now?" Henry asked.

"I believe that you are getting better at noticing desperation on others but I'm not sold on the idea that you have psychic powers just yet," Jill said.

"Maybe we should all go over and talk to the woman," James said. "Or maybe you could say something Jill; it's less weird if a woman does it. You could say something like, are there any bathrooms on this train?"

"We already know that there are no bathrooms on this train, which again is ridiculous when you consider it," Jill said. "But I normally I don't like talking to people that I don't know."

"Well okay Jill but it's your loss, a chance to maybe expose a woman as desperate," Henry said. "Or maybe you're just afraid that I will be proven right."

"If I go over and talk to the woman do you promise that you will shut up about this," Jill said.

"I promise I will shut up for a while," Henry said.

"Fine, good enough," Jill said as the three of them slowly walked over to the woman and started standing next to her. Jill smiled and nodded at the woman next to her before reluctantly deciding to introduce herself. "Hi my name is Jill."

"Elizabeth," the woman said sounding like she didn't exactly want to be having an instance of conversation either.

Jill was thinking that maybe she should not say anything but then Henry and James noticed that she was sort of standing there awkwardly and not saying anything.

"Do you still have to go to the bathroom Jill?" James asked out of the blue.

"I don't have to go to the bathroom," Jill said as she very slowly and carefully pressed her knees together as well as the rest of her legs to try and take some of the pressure off of her bladder.

"Jill's just shy but she didn't want to admit it, do you know if there any bathrooms around here?" Henry asked.

"I wish, I could surely use one right now," Elizabeth said as she laughed causing Jill to laugh as well.

James shook his head. "You women always seem to have to go to the bathroom."

"Well maybe if they gave us more bathrooms we wouldn't find ourselves in these emergency situations," Jill said shaking her head. "Not that I am in an emergency situation or anything."

"Well I certainly am," Elizabeth said as she laughed. "I haven't gone to the bathroom all day; you can't find a bathroom in the city if your life depended on it."

"You're telling me," Jill said as she looked at her watch to realize that there was still a long way to go until they would be home.

Jill couldn't help but notice that Elizabeth was shifting from leg to leg and watching her desperate was making her more desperate. She couldn't help but notice that James and Henry were looking at her every so often and smirking. Once again she wanted to say something to them but she knew that she couldn't say anything without admitting she had to go to the bathroom and she wasn't about to do that.

Several stops went by and more people got on and off the train, more people getting on than off. Jill carefully watched James and Henry as they looked at all of the women getting on the train and she was thinking that they must be assessing all of them. In fact she noticed that every time that they were looking at a woman if she looked closely enough she could tell that the woman seemed to be showing telltale signs of leg shifting, foot tapping and other signs of bladder agitation.

"There's a whole lot of red and orange on this train," James said as he laughed.

Elizabeth looked around and didn't see much red or orange on the train and shrugged her shoulders.

"It's a guy thing, their secret code, they've been doing it all day and being highly immature about it," Jill said as she crossed and uncrossed her legs and leaned up against the wall to try and take a little bit more of the pressure off.

But Jill couldn't help but start looking around the train and looking at all the women thinking of just what she could do if she had such an ability. She was starting to think that maybe the guys did have something that she didn't have. She thought she was good at spotting people who were desperate to pee but they were seemingly able to identify woman who needed to go without them showing any obvious signs. Maybe they were improving in noticing desperation but now it seemed like they were prodigies, noticing people and things that even Jill didn't see any sign of.

As the train faced some delays and the ride got bumpier Jill gritted her teeth and started frowning and becoming agitated. She looked at her watch and it seemed like time had slowed down as her bladder grew fuller and fuller by the moment.

Finally the train opened at their stop and Jill was practically ready to bolt out of the train and immediately went towards the bathroom and got in line. Elizabeth got in line right behind her with a very frantic and frenzied look on her face. She knew that look, she had maintained her composure the entire train ride but now that she was near relief the urge was becoming even more overwhelming.

"I thought you didn't need to go to the bathroom Jill?" Henry said with a laugh.

"And you sure don't look mellow yellow," James said.

"Well I figure I should just go to the bathroom as like a precaution," Jill said not wanting to admit that she was struggling with every fiber of her being to hold it in.

"Well if you don't have to go that bad you should let Elizabeth go in front of you since I think that she has to go pretty badly," Henry said.

"Yeah that would be the nice thing to do," James said.

Now Jill was becoming absolutely furious but she didn't want to seem like a bitch so she simply smiled and nodded. "Go ahead Elizabeth, it's okay," Jill said as Elizabeth stepped in front of her.

"Thank you dear, it's nice to see that some people are still concerned about their fellow human beings," Elizabeth said.

Henry and James stood there under the pretext that they were waiting for Jill but enjoying every moment of the line where they could see that tons of women coming off the train who really needed the bathroom badly. Finally Jill went into the bathroom door and after hearing Elizabeth having one of the longest loudest pees of her life Jill practically pushed her out of the way and slammed her ass down on the toilet and just made it at the last second.

When Jill finally came out of the bathroom Henry and James

simply smiled and began laughing.

"Oh shut up you guys are so immature, if there's anyone on the earth who should listen to the phrase with great power comes great responsibility it should be you guys," Jill said.

"We did use our power responsibly, we convinced you to let that woman go ahead of you," James said. "Because like you said you didn't have to go to the bathroom that badly right?"

"Right," Jill said shaking her head.

"Well now you are looking pretty white," James said.

"Of course I am, I'm Scandinavian and I hardly ever get out during the day," Jill said as the three of them laughed.

But as the three of them walked away from the train station and Jill thought about the events of the day another chill went up her spine as she started to think, not so much in the back of her mind anymore, but more towards the forefront, that maybe, just maybe these guys were on to something, and that did not fare well for Jill in the future.

When Jill got home and sat down on her bed that night and looked at the ceiling she simply shook her head once more. "I wish I had eaten those rancid ass tacos," she said as she closed her eyes and went to sleep.

8

The next day Jill went over to see Henry and James in order to admit what she would rather not admit but now she was too insanely curious not want to investigate further.

"Okay I'll bite, I'm not saying that I fully believe you yet, but after everything I saw in the last couple of days I am willing to at least entertain the idea that you might have some type of psychic ability or maybe the you have just become really good at spotting desperate women in a way that even I cannot do," Jill said.

"Well that's very humble of you Jill," Henry said. "It takes a lot of maturity to admit that your friends might have some type of power or ability that you simply don't. We are just better at spotting desperate women than you and it's through no fault of your own, we just happen to have extraordinary psychic powers and you do not."

"Well once again you're kind of rubbing it in like you do when there is a bathroom line for me and none for you," Jill said shaking her head.

"I think that someone is just jealous and they don't want to admit it," James said.

Jill tried to restrain herself but she couldn't any longer. "God dammit why don't I have special psychic abilities?! I ate food from that disgusting carnival just like you guys, how come I don't have any magical powers? I mean granted it's not the same as having x-ray vision or controlling magnetism or the weather like the X-Men do, but I still think would be a pretty awesome power to know exactly how badly other women have to go to the bathroom. It just doesn't make sense that you would gain the exact psychic ability that is perfectly suited to all your own personal perversions."

"And again they are your personal perversions as well and you are just jealous, at least admit that," James said.

"I just don't get it, why would you get this specific power like this though," Jill said shaking her head. "I mean I'm acknowledging that I'm jealous and that this is totally awesome that you have this power, but it still doesn't make sense that you have this power, know what I am saying? I mean how does eating some tacos and getting sick from that give you suddenly the ability to read people's auras but only specifically in regards to how bad women have to go to the bathroom?"

"Maybe we actually do have other psychic powers," Henry said. "Maybe this is just the tip of the iceberg. Maybe the only reason we have realized this specific power is just because this is what is most interesting to us. Perhaps we can read auras in general and we are just reading how badly women have to go to the bathroom because that's what our perverted filthy minds are tuned into."

"I have to admit the ability seems a little bit sexist," Jill said shaking her head. "I mean why is it only women that you can tell how badly have to go to the bathroom?"

"I have no idea Jill," Henry said. "Maybe it has something to do with women's desperation aura. Maybe a woman with a full bladder gives off an aura of desperation in a way that a man doesn't."

"When is the last time you have ever been desperate," Jill said. "The only time a guy ever gets desperate is if he specifically chooses to. Oh I acknowledge that occasionally a man will be genuinely desperate to use the bathroom but generally speaking you will be able to find one, and failing that you will just go pee outside."

"That's true," James said as he high-fived Henry once again. "I have to admit it is kind of good being a guy, specifically a guy with the ability to know when women have to go to the bathroom."

"Did you ever think about the ethical implications of the fact that you are invading someone's privacy by seeing how badly they have to go to the bathroom," Jill said.

"Once again you're just being jealous," James said. "You're only worrying about the ethical implications of it now because you don't have the ability and you want to try and limit our fun out of jealousy."

"I suppose it does have profound ethical ramifications," Henry said shaking his head. "But it's not like we chose to have this ability. I mean don't get me wrong, I am totally psyched that we have this ability, but it's not like we can turn it off. It's probably a good thing that at least we enjoy this ability because the people who didn't like this ability, well they would probably not like the fact that every woman they see is glowing. You can't penalize us for looking at people because it's unavoidable. The aura is just there now and it's something that we can't avoid. You can't help but notice it, so if I happen to be looking at a woman and her aura is glowing red I'm not specifically invading her privacy, but I also can't just ignore the fact that I know she is bursting to go to the bathroom and ready to explode."

"Yeah but when you see that she is ready to explode I'm sure that you are ready to explode in another sense of the word," Jill said rolling her eyes.

"True that," James said as he once again high-fived Henry. "But the thing is now that we have this ability and we don't know how long it's going to last, we should try to maximize its potential while we still can. What is the absolute best place we could possibly go to see the most desperate women in one single place?"

Henry and James looked at Jill who pointed to herself. "Oh so now you guys need my expertise like at that carnival that we went out where you obtained your magical powers."

"But let's not call our powers magical, they could just be a naturally occurring phenomenon with nothing supernatural about them," James said. "Although on the other hand it is pretty cool that

I could have magical powers, it makes me almost like Harry Potter."

"The Harry Potter of female desperation," Jill said. "I could see that as a book, Harry Potter and the Bursting Bladder Female."

"Oh cool, imagine if I had something like a magic wand and all that I had to do was point to this or that woman and I could make her desperation grow," James said. "I mean again don't get me wrong, it's great that we have these powers, but wouldn't it be great if we could also alter the level of desperation? Like if we really concentrated we could make a woman's desperation level go up?"

"Well now you are just getting positively greedy," Jill said. "Although I would admit that it would be pretty cool if not for the fact that I know you guys would use that against me."

James closed his eyes and started rubbing the temples of his forehead as he stared at Jill and started muttering stuff.

"What the hell are you doing now?" Jill asked shaking her head.

James opened his eyes and looked at Jill and shook his head. "Nope, it doesn't seem like you are any more desperate just from me using my psychic powers to try and make your desperation level higher. You are still just white with little droplets of yellow."

"A very interesting turn of phrase," Jill said. "But yes I am only at white or yellow or mellow yellow or whatever the hell you want to call it by your color coding system, because as always I went to the bathroom before I came here. The only way my desperation level is going to rise as if I keep drinking and avoid the bathroom, which you know I'm obviously not going to do, probably even less so now that I know you guys have the ability to read me psychically."

"But the question remains, where can we best utilize our powers for the common good of humanity?" Henry asked.

"And by the common good of humanity you mean that you want to get your rocks off," Jill said. "Let's not pretend that you are Albert Schweitzer here, I don't think that there is any humanitarian potential behind this ability. Again I'm not denying that I am jealous that you have the ability, I'm just saying that unless you really like knowing when women have to go to the bathroom it's a pretty useless ability."

"Again totally jealous," James said. "But if this power is not going to last forever I do want to get the maximum use out of it while we still can. So where should we go Jill?"

Jill scratched her chin. "Well you know there's that big amusement park that is just opening and you know that those places always have inadequate female restrooms, well technically speaking pretty much every place on the face of the planet does, but those places are especially bad because there are huge numbers of people and only a few toilets."

"An amusement park!" Henry said as he stood up. "You know what I think that is a pretty good idea. Amusement parks have long lines for rides, long lines for bathrooms, lots of food and drink and an inadequate number of bathrooms. That will give us ample opportunities to see women who not just have to go to the bathroom really bad but who might be stationary for long stretches of time."

"I'm both impressed and a little bit nervous the amount of thought that you have put into this," Jill said. "But you know what, I am totally on board, let's go to the amusement park. I am sure that it will be a really fun type of event for us to test out this new power of yours."

"Oh we've been testing it out all along Jill," Henry said. "Now we want to go for the glory, for one of the big-time events. The grand opening of this new amusement park I think is the perfect opportunity. So shall we plan for tomorrow?"

"Sounds like a plan," Jill said.

The next day they all woke up bright and early so that they could get to the amusement park for the grand opening. Jill made sure specifically not to drink too much and to go to the bathroom before they ended up leaving because as much as she was enjoying the prospect of seeing lots of desperate women she didn't really relish the possibility of being one. Of course she knew that she would have to use the bathroom at some point during the day but she was hoping that maybe she would be able to sneak off without the guys noticing.

"Well Jill I can see that you are here bright and glowing this morning," James said as they picked up Jill.

"Well right now she's just like a white light so I suppose that she probably just went to the bathroom, but that will change, and we will know it," Henry said.

As Jill got in the car she had to admit that she did feel

awkward knowing that they could tell how badly or not she had to go to the bathroom. As she thought harder about it she realized that there wouldn't be any possibility of hiding it from them. And as soon as they could see that her bladder was building up they would probably keep trained on her like a hawk and not let her out of their sights.

But Jill didn't want to worry about that right now, she would worry about it when the time came. There was a long line to get into the amusement park but it was worth it because the guys spotted at least one woman on line who seemed to be doing a pee dance. As soon as she paid her admission she ran through the gates and probably bolted first thing to the bathroom.

"So boys how does the landscape look," Jill said as she put her arms around them and looked from side to side.

"I have to admit it's a virtual sea of rainbow colors," Henry said. "The fact is with this many women you're going to have a wide diversity of bladder sizes and liquid consumption. But hey that's what keeps the hunt interesting."

"Once again I would rather you not refer to this as the hunt because that sounds really creepy and stalker-ish," Jill said as she shook her head.

"Well let me use my Terminator scan to see who has to go to the bathroom," Henry said as he looked up and down. "There's one, come with me if you want to pee or see someone who has to pee."

"That wasn't the best improvised Terminator line," Jill said as she shook her head again. "But okay, if you have found someone worth following around I guess we can discreetly start following her around."

"It's that one," Henry said as he pointed to a young woman about Jill's age who seemed to be shifting from leg to leg.

"I can confirm that," James said.

"Well even I can confirm that, it's obvious from the way she is dancing that she has to go to the bathroom," Jill said. "See I can still tell that even without phenomenal psychic powers."

The three of them begun following around the woman, who was a rather petite brunette woman. Jill had to admit that the woman actually did look a lot like herself, which almost made her feel self-conscious.

"How's the glowing coming?" Jill said.

"If you could see what we see right now you would realize that she is at red alert," Henry said. "I can't believe that she hasn't left to find a bathroom yet."

"Speaking of which where are the bathrooms?" Jill said before she realized that she didn't want to admit that she was actively concerned where the bathrooms were.

"What's the matter Jill, feeling a bit blue?" James said as he and Henry laughed.

"Well she certainly isn't mellow yellow anymore," Henry said.

"Hey shut up," Jill said. "But if I understand your color coding system correctly blue isn't exactly desperate you know."

"Yeah but you are starting to get there Jill," James said. "It's only a matter of time before you go from blue to green to orange to red."

Jill hated to admit that they were 100% right about that but she wasn't about to say anything like that.

"Hey let's focus on red alert over there," Jill said as she pointed to the woman who now seemed to be walking away. "It looks like our prey is getting away from us. God dammit now you've got me referring to her in creepy stalker-ish terms."

They followed the woman until they seemed to be in a crowd of women that were walking in the opposite direction.

"Wow this is an entire group full of reds and oranges," Henry said.

"What do you mean?" Jill asked"

"He means that all of the women walking in the opposite direction of the woman that we have been following are all red and orange, meaning that they all have to go to the bathroom."

"I wonder why there are so many women who are desperate to pee walking this way?" Jill said shaking her head. "I have to admit I fully believe you, all of those women look extremely agitated."

"I think I know why," James said with a big smile as he pointed to the ladies room which had a big out of order sign on the door. "I think that this just made things a whole lot more interesting!"

"Not for me!" Jill shouted.

"Well Jill it looks like you are once again green with envy," James said as he began laughing and slapped Henry five. "But you are one of the only greens in a sea that is full of oranges and reds. I think that we should stay here and we can watch all of the women approaching the bathroom and then walking away disappointed that they didn't get to go."

Jill had to admit that now she was starting to panic. She started shaking her head and trying to act cool and collected about the whole thing. "Hey maybe there is another ladies bathroom around here, I mean a place this large can't possibly only have one ladies room."

Henry and James burst out laughing.

"Oh Jill you have lectured us enough to know that of course there can only be one ladies room here," James said. "Or in this case no ladies room I guess."

James and Henry began laughing again very loudly.

"It's not funny!" Jill shouted.

"You know what she's right, this isn't funny," Henry said as he looked down at the floor and shook his head before looking up and looking right at Jill. "It's freaking hilarious!"

"You guys are such assholes, already your power is going to your head!" Jill said.

"I know that the power is going to another head in my body," James said as he pointed to his crotch.

"And that's totally not creepy to do in public or anything," Jill said shaking her head.

"You're just mad because you are getting green with envy," James said. "And speaking of making you envious I think that it's time for me to go to drain the lizard in the men's room, which fortunately is not out of order."

"Yeah I think that I could probably use a drain on the main vein as well," Henry said.

"Have fun in the bathroom girls," Jill said shaking her head. "Honestly and they say girls always go to the bathroom in groups." But Jill just knew that they were doing it simply to annoy her and it was working. As she stood there staring at the ladies room with the out of order sign on it she couldn't help but notice that just seeing that was making her need to go more.

Jill quietly tiptoed over to the door to the ladies room and pushed on it. "Dammit, they locked it already! I have to admit that I was kind of hoping that they would have it unlocked. Even if the bathroom was out of order I could probably still use it quickly before the guys even came out."

"Hey Jill what are you doing," James said as he came out of the men's room.

"Holy Christ that was fast!" Jill shouted.

"It was," Henry said as he and James high-fived each other. "That's the greatness of having a penis."

"Are we going to go on some rides or something or are we just going to hang around in front of the empty ladies room all day?" Jill asked.

"Well it would be stupid to come to an amusement park and not go on any rides," James said shaking his head. "But on the other hand just seeing Jill looking longingly at that out of order ladies room is probably more satisfying to me than any type of ride and probably a bigger adrenaline rush as well."

"You see this is why I can't go places with you guys," Jill said shaking her head. "You have to be so immature about everything."

"Jealous!" they both said as they began laughing at Jill.

"Well I'm going to go on some rides," Jill said as she started walking away.

"We both know that she'll be back shortly," Henry said. "Even though she knows the bathroom was out of order we know that she will keep coming back to check on it."

Jill started wandering around the park as she started noticing her desire to urinate even more by the moment. Then she saw a ride with a rather long line to it and noticed that it was a water ride.

"Given my condition it would be idiotic to go on a ride like that," Jill said just as she suddenly had an idea. "Or rather a brilliant idea!"

Jill stood on line and she couldn't help but wonder how many women in the line had to go to the bathroom. But if her plan worked hopefully the guys would have no idea what she did. Even she didn't like to admit that she was thinking of going on the water ride seeing as if she was soaked anyway no one would notice if she peed herself. She figured it doesn't count as wetting yourself if you are already wet at the time.

However, just when she didn't want to see them the most, that was when Henry and James came over to her and got on line with her.

"You got in line for a water ride?" Henry said as he looked up and down the line. He then smirked. "I see what you're trying to do, trust me you're not the only one, lots of reds and oranges on this line."

"Desperate times call for desperate measures," Jill said as she pressed her legs together.

"Well you know Jill they finally opened the ladies room again," James said.

"They did?" Jill said as her eyes lit up. "Seriously?"

"Scouts honor," Henry said.

"Okay fine I'll just use the bathroom then," Jill said as she got off the line and followed Henry and James until she went up to the ladies room and saw that there was still an out of order sign on it which he pushed on and the door did not open. Jill turned angrily and glared at Henry and James.

"Did I mention that I got kicked out of the Boy Scouts?" Henry asked.

"And I never joined," James said as the two of them began laughing and high-fiving each other.

"Screw you guys," Jill said as she started walking away.

"Where are you going Jill?" Henry said with a smirk.

"Splashdown," Jill said as the two of them began laughing as Jill got back on line for the water ride. This time Henry and James got in line with her. "What are you guys doing?"

Henry shook his head. "Jill we wouldn't miss this for the world!"

Henry and James spent the next half hour while they were waiting in line enjoying every second of Jill bobbing up and down waiting until they were at the top of the mountain. The three of them got down on a raft which started cascading down the river splashing them all with water.

As the three of them got off the ride soaking wet Henry and James looked at Jill.

"In the clear!" the two of them said as they slapped each other five.

Jill began laughing.

What's so funny Jill; we were the ones who realized that you went to the bathroom while we were on the ride?" James said.

"Yeah but you guys sat in it," Jill said as she started to walk off.

Henry simply shook his head as he looked at James and smiled. "Well she's got us there!"

9

"But Jill it's a great idea!" Henry shouted.

"I don't know the whole idea sounds really weird, like not the good kind of weird, like the really awkward and disturbing kind of weird," Jill said. "Besides you're not the one who has to do all the work!"

"I think that he has a point Jill, you really have to look at this with an open mind," James said. "We finally found a way that we can possibly make money using our newfound psychic powers."

"Well I will hand it to you, I never thought that you would think of a way to find a way to make money off of being able to psychically predict when women are going to have to go to the bathroom," Jill said. "It did seem like an ability that pretty much had no real practical value aside from people like us who have a fetish for it."

"You see Jill, it's really a great idea," Henry said. "The thing is we know how badly any given woman has to go to the bathroom and how long before she is going to be not able to take it anymore. So all we have to do is get you into a bladder holding contest with a woman that we know is going to give up before you do. We will just find a woman who has to pee more than you and who has to pee faster than you and then you will just out hold her and we will put bets down on who will last the longest and we will really rake it in."

"I know it's just I feel really weird at the idea of having a holding contest with a woman that I don't even know," Jill said.

"What's the matter, are you afraid that you are going to lose?" James asked.

"No it's just a lot of pressure," Jill said.

"Hee hee pressure," Henry said. "As in bladder pressure!"

"It's not just a matter of bladder pressure it's also a matter of social pressure," Jill said shaking her head. "When you are sitting there with a bursting bladder trying to maintain your composure and knowing that people are watching you, well it's pretty damn intimidating!"

"Come on Jill this is basically foolproof," Henry said. "The thing is that we have an ace up our sleeves because we are going to know how badly other women have to go to the bathroom versus how badly you have to go to the bathroom, so we have an unfair advantage of knowing who's going to have to end up peeing first. It's really brilliant in its simplicity."

"Well then we'd better keep you guys out of Vegas because you'll get kicked out for counting bladders," Jill said shaking her head. "This whole idea does still sound ridiculous though, you realize that. I mean where are you even going to find women who want to engage in some bladder holding challenge while everybody takes bets on us?"

"You just leave that up to me," James said as he nodded and smiled. "But come on Jill, to have a power like this and not use it for personal gain, why it would be a crime not to use a gift like that. It would be like if Picasso decided that he wanted to become a musician instead or decided that he only wanted to paint caricatures on a board walk or something like that. We have a profoundly amazing new power to know when women have to pee and how badly and how long before they become unbearably desperate. If we don't exploit this for financial gain, well frankly it's un-American."

"I really feel that I'm going to regret this," Jill said as she shook her head. "Like I mean I feel like this is going to be probably one of the most awkward and embarrassing situations of my life."

"You know you say that a lot when you are with us," Henry said.

"Gee I wonder why," Jill said as she rolled her eyes.

"Don't worry I have the perfect location for something like this," James said. "I think that we will find plenty of people who will be willing to take up our little challenge."

"Once again, I'm the one who has to do all the work while you just have to sit there and watch," Jill said shaking her head. "But fine, I can see that you're not going to drop this until we give it a try but we split the money three ways, or you know what we should split 40/30/30 as I think I deserve a little bit more since I'm going to be the one suffering all the bladder pain."

"But we're like the amazing bladder twins," James said. "We're the ones with all the special magical powers of which we know you are still extremely jealous."

"Okay whatever, let's just get this over with," Jill said.

That weekend they went to the park where they set up a small table with a sign that read take the bladder buster challenge.

"This still feels ridiculous," Jill said as she sat at the park bench. "I mean even if you are able to tell if a woman has to go to the bathroom more than I do how do you know that she is going to fill up as quickly or not as quickly or whatever?"

"Jill I think that you are overthinking this," Henry said.

"By overthinking it you mean I am pointing out the potential flaws in your well-placed plans that I am going to have to bear the brunt of."

"We have it covered Jill," James said. "The fact is that everybody comes into the bladder buster challenge with a certain amount of urine in their bladders. And the fact also is that we know you haven't been drinking that much today in an effort to keep your bladder empty and that you went to the bathroom not long ago. So what we need to do is we need to find a woman who's already at stage green or higher so she will be starting with a bladder that is already somewhat uncomfortable. We can lie and tell her that you have been drinking a little bit so that she will think that you are equally matched but not knowing that you have a bladder that is closer to empty."

"Yeah but what if she questions whether our bladder strengths are not equal or wants us to start off at the same level or something like that," Jill said shaking her head. "There's just so much that I am thinking of that could interfere with your plans."

"I think that Jill might have a point," Henry said. "Maybe what we need to find is a woman who is not as questioning as Jill is."

"You mean we need to find an airhead?" James asked. "Well I think that most women are not as questioning as Jill."

"I'm not sure if I should take that as a personal complement or a sexist remark against all women," Jill said. "But I think I agree with your point actually. If we find a woman who wouldn't ask these types of questions it would be easier to trick her into our little scheme. Do you see any full bladdered girls or filling bladder girls that don't look like they are anywhere near as intelligent as me? Although to be fair I think that most women aren't as intelligent as me, most men too."

"How humble," Henry said as he started looking around. He spotted a woman with thick glasses and a bladder that didn't look very full. "Okay not her." Then he saw another woman without glasses but whose bladder seemed only like it was at level yellow. "Not her either, too close to even with Jill." He continued looking around until he saw a a blonde girl blowing gum and giggling excessively at everything the guy she was with was saying. Henry looked at her bladder to see that she was already at stage green. "Bingo."

"You found one?" Jill asked.

"Look at blondie there," Henry said as he pointed over to her. "Now I don't want you to accuse me of stereotyping all blondes as airheads, but she is looking kind of –"

The blonde girl began giggling and popping her gum as she snapped some selfies of herself with a tree.

"Yeah she's not winning any scholarships," Jill said as she nodded. "But how is her bladder?"

"Well she's definitely in the green zone," Henry said. "And since you are still at white with just specks of yellow since you went to the bathroom not long ago I think that this is probably our best bet, both in terms of the fullness of her bladder and the ease of which we can convince her to compete with you without her probably asking you any type of questions."

Jill looked at the blonde girl. "She doesn't really look desperate. I mean she's not crossing her legs, she's laughing and looks really casual and everything."

"Well she's not at the desperation stage yet but she's a lot closer to it than you are and not everybody shows it as much. But look at it this way, if you are starting pretty close to empty and she is already at the stage where she must be feeling the pressure in her bladder, once the two of you start drinking she's going to fill up a lot faster than you, so by the time you get to level green she will probably be practically wetting her pants."

"I sure hope so," Jill said shaking her head. "Because you know I'm definitely not going to wet my pants. If I get to the point where I am in agonizing pain I am going to concede and run for the bathroom."

"I'm telling you Jill this is a sure thing. James you can

confirm it right?"

"He's totally telling the truth Jill, she's obviously at the green level so even if she isn't showing obvious signs of desperation she can't hide the fact that her bladder is rapidly filling from us."

"Okay fine, why don't you get them over here," Jill said as she stared at the blonde girl who was still taking pictures of herself popping her gum in front of a tree.

"Hey," Henry said as he waved over to the blonde girl and her boyfriend motioning for them to come over. The guy came over with his girlfriend wondering what he was motioning for him for. "I am Henry, and these are my friends James and Jill."

James and Jill waved at them.

"We were wondering if maybe you would like to accept our challenge," Henry said as he pointed to the bladder buster sign. "Basically what we want to do is we want to see you two have a pee holding contest."

"Who me and her," the guy said pointing to Jill.

"No the two women," Henry said. "It wouldn't be fair to have a guy and a girl compete against each other. What were your names?"

"I'm Mark and she's Britney," Mark said as he pointed to the blonde girl.

"I was named after Britney Spears," Britney said as she popped her gum and continued chewing. "So you want the two of us to see how long we can hold our pee?" Britney began laughing and giggling like crazy. "That's the funniest thing in the world."

"Of course we would want to speed this up so that these two girls would be drinking a whole damn lot," James said as he pointed to numerous cans of soda on the table.

"How much would we be betting?" Mark asked. "Because I can tell you I totally have faith in my girl here." He pulled Britney closer she smiled and giggled some more.

"I guess we could bet something like $50 each," Henry said. "I was hoping that maybe we could get a whole bunch of people to come and maybe put money into the pot. The more money you put in the more money you will get out."

"That sounds like a good idea," Mark said. "Okay I will put down $50 both for myself and for Britney here."

"Actually let's make it $60," Henry said as he pointed to

himself James and Jill. "That's easier for us to split three ways."

"Okay so we have settled on that and now maybe some more people will come and start putting money into the pot on who they are betting for," Henry said.

"Okay ladies, start drinking," James said as he put two sodas down in front of Jill and Britney as they both opened their sodas.

"Bottoms up," Jill said as she held up her soda to Britney.

"Cheers," she said as she clinked her soda can against Jill's soda can and the two of them began drinking.

"We will have them drink one can every five minutes," James said. "And the first one to give up and run to the bathroom or to wet their pants loses."

Britney and Jill started rapidly downing the sodas as more people showed up to place their bets on which girl they thought was going to be able to hold the longest.

For the first couple of sodas it didn't seem like much was happening but more and more people started coming over intrigued by what was going on, and soon the pot was growing. Henry and James became the virtual bookies writing down everyone's bets and putting the money in the pot.

"What if we want to change our bets?" a guy in the audience asked. "Like what if we see one girl seems like she is losing and we want to change our bets can we do that?"

"I guess so," James said. "I mean I think that they're both pretty equally matched as they are both drinking the same amount of soda." James looked at Jill carefully and that's when he noticed that she was now at stage yellow with flickers of blue but that Britney was still holding at a solid green.

"Feeling the pressure yet?" Jill asked.

"Nope I'm good," Britney said as the two of them drank another soda.

The two of them sat there staring at each other both sitting fairly still as a crowd started gathering around them.

"Come on up and place your bets," James said acting like a virtual showman. But as he looked at Jill he noticed that she was now approaching stage blue while Britney was still only at green and not getting worse.

"How are you doing," Jill asked as she finished her next soda.

"I'm doing fine, how about you?" Britney said with an evil smirk.

"I'm mellow yellow," Jill joked.

"Actually I think she's feeling rather blue," Henry said to James.

"Yeah I noticed," James said. "She's filling up rather quickly."

The two of them continued drinking until it had been a half hour. By now Jill was noticing that she definitely had to go to the bathroom and it was getting harder and harder to ignore. Despite the fact that she seemed like an airhead Britney seemed like she was a bit more observant than they maybe gave her credit for.

"You look like you are frowning," Britney said. "I hope that the pressure's not getting to you."

"Not at all," Jill said as she tried to adjust herself in her seat a little bit.

James waved Henry over to an out-of-the-way area. "I think that Jill is in trouble, she is now very solidly up to green so now she is equally matched with Britney but Britney hasn't gone up the entire time."

"I know, what are we going to do?" Henry asked.

"Let's just wait and see what happens," James said.

They continued watching until the contest had been going on for 50 minutes now as Britney and Jill both began belching.

"Excuse me," Jill said.

"Me too," Britney said as she began giggling like an idiot again.

"It looks like we are almost out of sodas," Jill said as she shifted around in her seat trying to not show any obvious signs of desperation but she didn't even notice that she was subtly crossing her legs and twitching around a little bit.

"Well folks it looks like they have finished the sodas so I guess we just have to wait for all of that liquid to hit their bladders," James said with laughter, but it was nervous laughter because he saw that Jill was now solidly orange and Britney was still at green and looking pretty cool and collected.

James pulled Henry over to the side again. "Okay this isn't looking good for Jill or the little wager that we have made."

"What do you think we should do?" Henry asked.

"Well I think that Jill will be mad if she ends up losing and we end up losing all of our money so I think that she would understand if we took our combined $60 and –"

"You think that we should bet against Jill?"

"She's dying out there man, she is at level orange approaching red and Britney is still sitting there at a very comfortable green. I think that we didn't take something into consideration, everyone has different bladder sizes and the feeling of desperation is at least somewhat subjective. But what we know is that Britney, while she definitely has to pee, is not ready to explode. Look at Jill, she's trying to hide it but you can see that she is having trouble sitting still. She will be glad that we bet against her if she knows that it would save our money."

"I think Jill would be pretty mad though if we knew that we kept her holding in a losing contest."

"Yeah but we can't really let Jill know that. We have to keep up the illusion that this is a pretty evenly matched contest so that people keep putting money in."

"Hey guys can I see you for a moment," Jill said as she waved James and Henry over. "You know my favorite color is red, what is your favorite color?"

That was the code that Jill gave so that they could tell her what level that Britney was at during any point in the game without her knowing that they had a secret code.

"I think that we both like red," Henry said as James nodded in agreement. "Can't go wrong with red."

Jill smiled and nodded as she gave him thumbs up. "Sounds pretty good, I think that I am a fan of red as well."

"She's definitely in the red zone," Henry said to James who nodded nervously. "It's a good thing we decided to change our bets."

By now Jill could barely sit still and people were noticing that she was squirming in her seat and crossing and uncrossing her legs.

"Getting a little antsy," Britney said as she smiled and started blowing some more gum.

"No, of course not, I'm just getting a little restless from sitting around all this time," Jill said. "How about you, how long do you think that you could go for?"

Britney smiled. "I think that I have a better poker face than you. Hey I love that song." Britney took out her phone and started playing the Lady Gaga song Poker Face. As Britney started swaying back and forth to the music looking really calm and casual Jill could barely sit still and was practically shaking in her seat.

"I think that your girl is giving out," Mark said as Jill started feeling extremely self-conscious over the fact that everyone clearly could tell that she had to go to the bathroom and that it was driving her crazy.

"Hey I'm not going to give up that easily," Jill said as she bounced in her seat and began grabbing herself as she started hugging her legs with her arms.

"Well I hope that you don't have any plans, Britney probably won't pee for another six hours," Mark said as he began laughing.

"Six hours!" Jill shouted as she stood up as she knocked her knees together and began bending. "Screw that, I'm going to the fucking bathroom!"

Jill ran off screaming towards the bathroom as Britney started shouting that she was the winner.

"Out of my way!" Jill shouted as she ran into the bathroom, practically knocked down the woman coming out of the stall, slammed the door shut and barely had time to jerk her pants down and slammed her ass down on the seat before she started exploding. She screamed with sighs of great relief and then she came out and washed her hands. When she came out of the bathroom Britney was standing there with her hands on her hips smiling.

"Well Britney I'll hand it to you, you have some amazing bladder strength," Jill said. "Are you going to go to the bathroom now?"

Britney waved her hands and laughed. "No, I'll wait until I really have to go. But we will be home in three hours so I'm not going to use some gross ass public toilet. I don't know how you could possibly sit on those things!"

Jill had to admit that now she was blushing. "Hey when you gotta go you gotta go. Good game."

Jill and Britney shook hands and she went to join her companions.

"Well way to lose all of our money," Jill said as she went back over to Henry and James.

"Well Jill I think you're going to be both happy and angry at us," Henry said. "Do you want the good news first or the news it's going to piss you off?"

"Well let's go with the good news I guess," Jill said shaking her head. "So at least I will be able to enjoy the good news before I get pissed off at you guys."

"Well the good news is that we didn't lose all the money, in fact we made a lot of money," James said. "But that's because when we saw that you were obviously going to lose we decided to change our bets and decided to bet against you. We didn't want to destroy the illusion of a fair game so we just kind of lied to you and let you think that Britney was a lot more desperate than she was. But the truth is Jill that she was at a solid green the entire time. Even though she drank a butt load of soda I guess some people don't fill up as fast. You went from zero to exploding in the time it took her to not even go up one color. I think that we have seen a flaw in our little plan. Although our powers can show us how desperate a woman is to go to the bathroom it can't tell us how long it's going to take her to get more desperate. We can only see how desperate she is at the moment and make an estimate. But Britney, she may have a head full of air, but she has a bladder of steel!"

"I have to say that this was a rather humiliating defeat and I knew something would go wrong," Jill said. "But let's swallow our pride and go home."

The three of them got in the car and then a couple of minutes later it inevitably happened as they pulled into the nearest gas station and Jill got out.

"Sorry but I broke the seal!" Jill shouted as she scampered towards the bathroom.

Henry and James looked at each other and burst out laughing.

"You know what between seeing Jill frantic like this and the fact that we still managed to cut our losses and make a profit, this was a pretty good day," James said.

"I'll toast to that," Henry said as he opened a soda and started drinking just as Jill got back in the car. "Want one?"

Jill gave a look of horror and shook her head. "You know what, I'm good."

Henry and James burst out laughing again and they continued laughing all the way on the very long ride home.

10

"So where shall we now demonstrate our awesome power," Henry said.

"There are so many possibilities, the world is basically our oyster," James said. "Do you have any thoughts on this Jill?"

"My bladder still hurts from the other day when you got me involved in that contest and lied to me about the fact that I was losing until I came dangerously close to wetting myself in public," Jill said as the two of them began laughing hysterically. "It's not funny! My bladder is really sore."

"Next time we just have to find a woman who we know has inferior bladder strength to Jill, even though Jill has a little girl bladder," Henry said.

"I bet I could probably out hold the both of you bozos, mostly because as a woman I often have to whether I want to or not."

"Are you challenging us to a contest Jill?" James asked.

"No, I am saying next time if you want to make money off of this ability you should be the ones doing all the holding," Jill said shaking her head. "Maybe you guys could experience some horrible bladder pain once in a while."

"I thought you said that you weren't interested in seeing men desperate to pee?" Henry asked.

"I'm not sexually turned on by it but it would be nice to see you suffer once in a while," Jill said.

"She's still jealous," they both said as they laughed and slapped each other five.

"I really wish I had eaten that rancid ass taco like you guys did," Jill said as she shook her head. "And I don't even really like tacos."

"But as a lesbian don't you like eating out lady tacos?" James asked as he smirked.

"You guys are so immature, it's not fair that you should get such an amazing power when you don't have the responsibility to use it responsibly," Jill said.

"Jealous," they both said again as they nodded.

"I am almost starting to wish that maybe you would end up losing the power," Jill said. "I'm getting kind of tired of you going on and on about it. And yes you're going to say I was jealous and yes I am jealous, but there's only so much you can do with a single power like that."

"Jill's right, we might end up losing the power someday, we don't know if it's just a temporary thing," Henry said. "Which again is all the more reason why we should use it to its maximum capacity while we still have it, that is why we have to find the best opportunities to use our power."

"Well there is this big outdoor festival coming up about an hour away from here," James said. "It's not like that small town carnival, I mean it's like a big huge thing with a concert and games and rides and food and lots of drinking."

"And with very few bathrooms or at least an inadequate amount," Henry said.

"That's pretty much every place when you're a woman, every place has an inadequate number of bathrooms for the number of women who need to use it," Jill said. "Besides, outdoor events, sure they have a lot of desperation but –"

"You're still bothered by the fact that we're going to know when you have to pee," Henry said as he laughed. "Well get used to it Jill, we might very well have this power forever so you won't be able to hide your desperation from us ever again."

"This is so not fair," Jill said as she shook her head. "I mean of all the worst people to get this devious power. But I suppose it could be worse, at least it's only you guys who have this power."

"Well we don't know that for sure Jill," James said. "Lots of other people might have eaten rancid ass tacos at that carnival."

"Don't you think we would have heard about that then?" Jill asked.

"Maybe not," Henry said. "The fact is it took us a while for us to even figure out what the power did. Even if someone else is experiencing this it's probably an unprecedented thing and people would probably dismiss it as some type of delusion or something like that. But it would be cool if we could find others with this power because then maybe we could figure out how to gain the power for other people and make sure that if this is a temporary condition we can maybe remake the formula so that we can continue knowing when women have to pee."

"And maybe I can eat some of it and I will have this awesome ability as well!" Jill said suddenly getting excited. "But how are we ever going to find other people who might have this ability? I think that even if we advertise it on the Internet the chances of us finding another person who has this ability and them just happening to come across our Internet posting are pretty slim to none. And quite frankly I'm afraid to find another person who has your abilities because that's just one more person who's going to know when I have to go to the bathroom."

"You always have to go to the bathroom Jill," James said.

"Not right now, and you know I'm telling the truth because you have a desperation lie detecting ability," Jill said.

"She's right, she's mellow yellow," Henry said. "But I think I like the idea of going to that big outdoor festival, it will be a great place to see lots and lots of excellent female desperation. With that many people and that few toilets you know that we will be having opportunities to watch it all night long."

"Yeah except you guys will be able to pee whenever you want and I will have to wait 45 minutes to go to the bathroom only to have to force my ass to make contact with those gross ass porta potties," Jill said as she shuddered.

"You could always hover over them," James said.

"Well that's just rude because it compounds the problem," Jill said before looking away. "Besides I don't know how to hover without pissing all over myself!"

The two of them burst out laughing.

"Hey shut up!" Jill said. "If you had to sit on some gross ass porta potty toilet seat you wouldn't be as eager to go."

"Yeah but we don't," James said as he slapped Henry five. "So are we agreed then, we're going to go to the big festival this weekend?"

Henry and James both looked at Jill with smiles on their faces.

"Come on Jill, we can't miss this as a wasted opportunity," Henry said. "Just don't drink a lot and maybe you can avoid having to use the bathroom."

Jill shook her head. "You know I think I have been drinking a whole lot less ever since you gained this ability, but I'm not going to dehydrate myself, and even if I minimize my drinking I'm still going to have to go to the bathroom."

"You'd be missing out on a lot," Henry said with a smirk.

"Okay fine I will go with you to the festival but I know I'm probably going to end up regretting it," Jill said as the two of them slapped each other five again.

The day of the big festival Jill made sure not to drink too much in the morning before she got on the bus but in the hour or more it took the bus to get there she had to admit that she was already up to level yellow with hints of blue. They noticed Jill frowning when they finally arrived after an hour and a half because of traffic and delays.

"What's the matter Jill, feeling blue," Henry said.

"Shut up!" Jill said.

"I'm feeling pretty blue myself," James said. "I think that when we finally get off the bus I'm going to go out into the field and go water the flowers. You should come with us Jill, it will save you a lot of time."

"I'm good," Jill said annoyed that she already had to go to the bathroom even if only a little bit. "Besides I'm not going to go blatantly exposing myself in public like you guys."

"Your loss," Henry said as he and James began laughing.

As soon as they got off the bus Henry and James went off to run into a nearby field to go relieve themselves as Jill waited patiently for them to return.

"Feeling better?" Jill said as they arrived back trying hard not to hide the fact that she was annoyed.

"We're running on empty," James said.

Jill shook her head. "It really must be nice when the whole world is your bathroom like that."

"It is," James said as he slapped Henry five again. "So I guess it's time for us to get looking. Hey I think I see someone who has to pee."

"Where?" Jill said.

"I'm looking at her right now, she seems pretty agitated," James said as he burst out laughing.

"Shut up, you know I'm not even desperate yet," Jill said as she shook her head.

"More so than we are," Henry said as he slapped James five yet again. "But she is right, we should find a woman who is already going out of her mind with desperation, Jill will get out of her mind with desperation soon enough."

Jill wanted to say something but she hated to admit that they were right. The fact that she already felt a slight urge to go to the bathroom and they had only just arrived meant that before long she would probably feel an ever-increasing urge that was hard to ignore. And they could already see that there were huge lines at the porta potties, disproportionately made up of women since they weren't going to go pee out in the open as often as the guys were.

"Hey there's one," James said as he pointed to a woman who was putting her hands on her knees and looking anxiously towards the lines at the porta potties.

"Even I can tell she's desperate just by looking at her," Jill said. "The strange thing is that your power only works on women so you wouldn't even know if other men were desperate would you?"

"Yeah but I also wouldn't care," Henry said.

"Not the least bit curious?" Jill asked. "I'm not really into male desperation but I still think it would be curious to know when men had to go to the bathroom, could potentially give you leverage in a situation. And guys are less obvious when they are desperate."

"Just admit it, we are better at holding and we don't go dancing around like little girls," Henry said as he started prancing around and laughing.

"It's true that women do a lot more dancing and squirming and body motions," James said.

"Yeah because that's all we've got, we can't just grab ourselves like you guys can," Jill said. "Crossing and uncrossing our legs and dancing around and hopping up and down is pretty much all we can do because that tension has to go somewhere."

"Also we rarely get desperate because we can pee basically anywhere," James said as he and Henry began laughing.

"You really like to remind me of that don't you," Jill said shaking her head.

"That's because we know it annoys the hell out of you, so now we have two advantages over you," James said. "Firstly we don't really get very desperate because we can pee wherever we want, and secondly we know when women are going to have to go to the bathroom but they don't know when we are going to have to go to the bathroom. It's a totally win-win situation for everyone but you Jill. Of course you do get to benefit from our amazing psychic powers because, lacking such powers yourself, you must rely on us to know when women are desperate to pee."

"Hey I can tell when women have to go to the bathroom, it's just not always as obvious because some people are more composed," Jill said. "In fact let me see if I can spot a desperate woman without using any fancy psychic powers."

Jill started looking around at women walking around but she had to admit that most of them weren't showing obvious signs of desperation. Finally she saw a woman who looked like she was a little bit agitated like something was on her mind.

"That woman might be desperate," Jill said as she pointed to a heavyset woman who was looking around like she was searching for something.

Henry shook his head. "Nope, she's mellow yellow, you have to go to the bathroom more than she does right now."

"I know but she looks really agitated by something like she is searching for something," Jill said as suddenly the woman's daughter came back to her and she shouted where the hell have you been and she replied that she had been at the bathroom and the lines were terrible.

"She was agitated because her daughter ran off to the bathroom," James said. "And hey the lines are terrible! This is looking to be a red letter day, or hopefully a red glowing day!"

"You see Jill that is what's great about our power, it's completely infallible," Henry said. "Body motion can be misleading. You thought that that big fat woman needed to pee really badly but she was just agitated because her daughter was taking a long time because she had to pee really badly. But the glow doesn't lie. A woman can show no outward signs of desperation yet she could be bursting on the inside and she can't hide it from us."

"Speaking of a red glowing day there is one right now," James said as he pointed to another woman who was standing around guzzling a drink but looking calm and cool and collected.

"She doesn't look like she has to pee at all," Jill said as she looked at the woman. "Look how casual she is and look how she's guzzling down those drinks like there's no tomorrow."

"Yeah but you didn't think that Britney looked very desperate either," James said. "But that's because desperation is somewhat subjective. Some people can be bursting at the seams but they can maintain their composure. Britney may have been a total airhead but she had good self-control when it came to controlling her bladder. You're also pretty good at concealing it, I'll give you that Jill, but right now we know that you are getting green with envy."

Jill didn't want to admit it but they were right, she was definitely feeling the urge to pee and it was getting hard to ignore. She wasn't quite desperate yet but she was getting a tad bit uncomfortable and was thinking about how much longer she could put off going to the bathroom.

"Okay I will grant you that, some people can deal with a hugely full bladder better than others without showing it so much," Jill said.

"But I think it is that our psychic gifts pick up on how much pressure there is in the bladder," James said. "Again I'm not a scientist and this admittedly doesn't sound very science-y, sounds kind of science fictional really or supernatural, but it seems like when a woman's bladder is full and experiencing the pressure of that full bladder that dictates what her glow is. The woman we are looking at right now may not be showing signs of desperation but I guarantee that she is ready to explode."

"If you say so," Jill said shrugging her shoulders. "Not having psychic powers I can't really say."

"Well there's one way to see if we are correct, and I am sure that we are," Henry said. "Let's just follow the bitch!"

Although Jill didn't like the idea of being like a stalker she had to admit that she was curious to see where this would lead so the three of them began subtly following the woman around.

"Wow she's glowing really bright red," Henry said. "I can't believe she's being so calm about it."

"If she is really as desperate as you say she is she should be in panic mode right now," Jill said. "She must have the bladder control of a goddess."

"I have to admit I am pretty impressed that this woman is managing to maintain her composure with a bladder this painfully full," James said. "I mean honestly Jill you seem more agitated than she is right now."

"Shut up!" Jill said as they noticed the woman started rapidly walking away. "She's getting away from us!"

The three of them followed the woman to notice that now she seemed to be speed walking.

"Now the hunt is on," Henry said.

"I still wish you wouldn't refer to it like that as it makes a sound like we are creepy predators," Jill said. "But I'll admit this is exciting."

"I can't wait until she sees the size of those lines; she might even have an accident!" James said.

When they said that Jill instinctively crossed her legs as she started thinking of just how long the lines were and measuring that against her own growing need for the bathroom. They continued watching and following the woman until they saw her run off into the field and she started looking around to see if anyone was nearby. The three of them decided that they would hide and pretend that they weren't looking at her. But that's when they saw it, the woman pulled down her skirt, squatted and began peeing in the bushes as a look of relief came over her face.

As Jill saw that woman getting relief she had to admit that her own need was now growing really rapidly and she couldn't help but notice that she was even shaking her leg a little bit.

"Wow look at her pee!" Henry shouted. "She has a really powerful stream."

"Yeah that's something," Jill said now tapping her foot a little bit.

"It looks like she's not the only one who needs relief," James said. "You're getting a little bit orange Jill."

"God dammit, you know when I have to pee and I see others going it just makes me worse," Jill said as she shifted around in place a little bit.

As the three of them were chatting and arguing that's when suddenly the woman started walking towards them looking displeased.

"Ooh, she doesn't look happy," Henry said as they saw the woman approach.

"Hey were the three of you watching me while I was going to the bathroom," the woman said.

"She was, she said that seeing you go made her have to go more," Henry said. "This is our friend Jill and she has to piss like a horse right now."

"Shut up!" Jill said. "I'm sorry we didn't mean to look at you, you just happened to be in our field of vision."

"Well you definitely got a good look," the woman said. "But hey I'm not inhibited, when you have to go you have to go, and it's better than waiting an hour in those ungodly lines."

"An hour," Jill said sheepishly.

"Hey if you want you can watch Jill pee, she's about to explode," James said as he laughed.

"That's not true," Jill said as she stomped her foot down angrily and began shaking it a bit. "Besides I can't go when people are watching!"

"If you want you can watch us pee," Henry said. "I think it's about time to drain the lizard again."

"Hey that doesn't sound so bad," the woman said. "I'm Janet by the way."

"I'm Henry, he's James, that's Jill," Henry said. "Now let's have a pee party! Sure you don't want to join us Jill?"

"No I'm good," Jill said as she pressed her legs together and realized that she was now in a terrible situation. Not only did she suddenly notice that she had to pee pretty badly but knowing that everyone else was going to the bathroom was aggravating her even further.

Jill turned her back as Henry and James went to pee in the field and came back a few minutes later.

"Your friends got a little bit pee shy but they still came through," Janet said smiling.

"Well there are a lot of women peeing in these fields," James said. "We could just stay here and watch all of these people peeing all day."

"Well that would be lovely except I really need to use the toilet right now," Jill said as she danced around in place.

"Good luck with that," Janet said as she put her arm around Jill's shoulders. "I'd sooner piss myself than use those disgusting dank ass toilets and wait an hour for the privilege."

"I'm sure they couldn't be that bad," Jill said frowning as she contemplated the situation she was in. Then it occurred to her that the big holding contest she did the other day probably weakened her bladder temporarily. "But either way I really need to get to a bathroom now."

Janet laughed. "Well then get in line sister; it's going to be a long wait."

"Well come on let's go," Jill said as she walked with a brisk pace until they got over to where the porta potties were. The line was snaking so long that she could barely even see the front of the line from the back of the line.

"Wow this line is full of glowing ladies," Henry said with a smile as he approached the line.

"Dammit why did I wait so long to get in line," Jill said. "Hey if you guys want to go and continue looking for other desperate women I would totally understand. You don't want to wait here for an hour with me do you?"

"Well Jill it would be rude to go off and leave you all alone," James said.

"Besides it will be fun watching you go from orange to red to supernova," Henry said.

"Dammit why don't these places have more bathrooms?!" Jill shouted. "And bathrooms that aren't so disgusting. I knew that something like this would happen if I came here. Well maybe the line will move more quickly."

"You keep telling yourself that Jill, it's not going to move the line along any faster," Henry said.

"And its one of those situations that I have a particular pet peeve about," Jill said as she tried to look ahead to the front of the line. "Multiple lines to multiple different porta potties, it should be first come first serve to whichever toilet opens up first. How many women are in this freaking line anyway?"

"Well it's a unisex line but we can always count," James said as he started walking along the line before coming back a minute or two later.

"So what's the good news?" Jill said as she gritted her teeth.

"Do you want the good news first or the bad news?" James said.

"What's the good news?" Jill said as she crossed and uncrossed her legs.

"Well the good news is that there are lots of reds and oranges in this line so we certainly won't be bored while we are waiting for you Jill," James said. "Are you sure you want the bad news?"

"Probably not," Jill said. "Is it as bad as it looks?"

"Worse. Do you even want to know how many people are ahead of you in line? Why don't you guess?"

"I'm going to be optimistic and guess maybe 30 people in line."

"You're 47th," James said as he laughed. "And most of the people in this line seem to be women, really desperate women."

"47th!" Jill said looking like her jaw was about to drop. "This is a nightmare."

"Hey for some of us it is a dream come true," Henry said. "We came here to see desperate women and now we are going to get to see them."

"Lovely," Jill said as she tried to look to the front of the line but it seemed as far off as the other side of the country.

"Oh Christ is this the line," another woman said as she got in the line next to Jill.

"I'm afraid so and we're both about 47th in line," Jill said to the woman.

"Holy crap I'm not even sure if I can last that long!" she said.

"Susan where are you," said a man as he walked over.

"I'm over here Dennis," the woman said as she waved to him.

"Well this is some line," Dennis said as he approached. "Well I guess you'll be waiting for a while Susan." He turned to Henry and James. "Are you guys waiting for one of your friends as well?"

"Yeah that's our friend Jill right next to your friend Susan," Henry said. "I'm Henry and my other friend here is James."

"Well it looks like both of our girls are in the red zone," Dennis said as he laughed.

"What do you mean by in the red zone?" James asked.

"I mean that they both wasted so much time getting in line that now they both have to pee really bad," Dennis said as he began laughing.

"It's not funny!" Susan and Jill both said simultaneously before they began laughing.

Dennis shook his head. "Women just can't control their bladders."

"Dennis seems to like watching me wait in line, he says that he has a sixth sense for when women have to go to the bathroom," Susan said. "He told me that I should have gotten in line a while ago. He has this weird notion that he can predict how badly a woman has to go to the bathroom simply by looking at them."

"What did you say?" Jill said as Henry and James looked at

each other with their eyes wide.

"Well hey, haven't I been right every single time," Dennis said. "It's the craziest thing, one day I just woke up and suddenly I was seeing all of these colors. It took me a while to figure out what the hell was going on but the crazy thing is that it seems that all these women seem to have a glow around them based on how bad they have to go to the bathroom."

"Holy fucking shit!" Henry shouted. "Dude, did you eat the tacos?"

"Did I what?" Dennis asked.

"You heard him, did you eat the freaking tacos?!" James said as he grabbed Dennis.

Dennis pushed him away. "What on earth are you talking about?"

"We have the same ability," Henry said as he pointed to himself and James. "We ate some rancid ass tacos, came down with a bad fever and then we woke up able to know how badly women have to go to the bathroom."

"You have to be freaking kidding me," Jill said as she put her hand on her forehead and started shaking her head back and forth. "This cannot be happening."

"What exactly is going on here?" Susan said as she shifted from foot to foot.

"Welcome to my nightmare," Jill said as she put her hand on Susan's shoulder.

"How on earth did you discover you had this ability?" Henry said. "How long have you had it?"

"Not that long," Dennis said. "I just woke up one morning and I noticed that I was seeing this weird glowing aura around women and then eventually I learned what it meant. And the funny thing is that I find it so entertaining to see women having to go to the bathroom."

"Dude so do we," James said as James, Dennis and Henry all slapped each other five.

"But you really didn't eat anything unusual or have a fever or anything?" Henry said.

"No, I just went to bed one night and I woke up and suddenly I started noticing that all the women I saw were glowing," Dennis said. "And it didn't take me long to realize that the glowing changed as that women needed to go to the bathroom. Susan fucking hates my ability though; she says it's really intrusive that I always know when she has to go to the bathroom. She tries to deny that I even have the ability but she knows that I am always right. It really has been enlightening."

"If you were really enlightened you would realize how uncomfortable this is!" Jill said as she crossed her legs tightly.

"Wow your friend really has to pee," Dennis said. "She probably has to pee even more than Susan."

"Don't blame Jill, she's just jealous that she doesn't have the ability," Henry said.

"Dennis is there anything strange that you did before you gained the ability," Jill asked.

Dennis shook his head. "No it just came out of nowhere. I went to sleep feeling normal maybe a little lightheaded at the most and then I woke up the next morning and bada bing bada bang I was suddenly endowed with amazing divine psychic powers."

"The three of you are all so humble about your newfound abilities," Jill said. "But what I want to know is where you got these abilities from? If it wasn't the tacos, then what was it?"

Dennis shrugged his shoulders. "Honestly I have no idea and I don't care, as long as I keep this ability I'm pretty happy."

"God dammit I want psychic powers too!" Jill said.

"Jill enjoys desperation but then she always gets annoyed when she finds herself in situations like this," Henry said.

"You wouldn't be happy if you were standing in line feeling on the verge of pissing yourself!" Jill said as she hopped from foot to foot.

"That's true, but we're not the ones on line on the verge of pissing ourselves so it's actually pretty funny," James said. "But don't worry Jill the line is moving, you were 47th but now you are like 42nd I think."

"Kill me now!" Jill said as she pressed her legs tightly together.

"Your friend is very entertaining," Dennis said. "Hey did you ever try making money using the ability?"

"Actually we had this foolproof plan for a pee holding contest but then Jill screwed it up by not having sufficient holding ability," Henry said.

"I screwed it up," Jill said as she bent at the knees. "You were the ones who pretty much thought that you knew exactly how desperate a woman was but then the woman that you picked had greater bladder capacity than me. I told you the whole thing wouldn't have worked out well."

"Well hey why don't you give us a second chance to prove it," Henry said. "Hey Dennis, why don't we wager on our girls?"

"You're going to bet on us, for what?" Jill asked. "We're not having a pee holding contest, we are stuck waiting in line, so whoever gets to the front of the line first will be going to the bathroom first."

"Hey she has a point," James said. "And since we all have amazing psychic powers everything would be equally balanced. Hey about this, let's bet to see which one of our girls will get to the head of the line quickest. See this way Jill can't screw it up because it's left to fate and fate alone."

"I didn't screw things up!" Jill shouted.

"Yeah Jill but you tend to have bad luck as well, so even in matters of fate I'm not sure if I want to bet money on you," Henry said.

"Hey I'm not bad luck," Jill said. "Why do you think that I am bad luck?"

"Well think of it this way Jill," Henry said as he scratched his head and looked at the line. "Would you say that you are in a lucky situation right now?"

Jill scratched her head and thought for a moment. "Okay point taken, but this is still mostly your fault for talking me into doing this."

"Well be glad I did, now we found another person with amazing psychic power," Henry said as he put his arm around Dennis. "Our good friend Dennis here. So Dennis would you be up for a friendly wager, Susan against Jill, to see who gets to go to the bathroom first? I'm even willing to make the wager even knowing that Jill's bad luck."

"I'll take that bet!" Dennis said as he shook Henry's hand.

"Now I know how the horses at the racetrack feel," Jill said. "Frankly this is dehumanizing to us both."

"Hey Jill you know that if you were on the outside of the line looking in you probably would have the opposite attitude so don't be a hypocrite about it," Henry said.

"Hey maybe it will pass the time," Susan said as she stepped forward a pace. "Hey I'm in the lead!"

"See Jill you're bad luck for me already," Henry said.

"Don't worry Jill you are up to 37th in line already," James said. "I am sure that the time will just fly by. And hey at least even if you lose we will all have good fun with it."

"Hey I'm up to 34th," Susan said as she stuck her tongue out at Jill from the line next to her.

"Don't worry I will catch up soon enough," Jill said.

15 minutes later.

"I don't even see Susan anymore," Jill said as she tried looking ahead. "Hey no fair, I think that her line has more men in it."

"Yeah I hadn't considered that when I made this bet," Henry said as he shook his head. "But don't feel bad Jill, I won't blame you if you lose, I knew I was taking a risk betting on a bad luck charm like you."

"Hey I would like to say that I hope that you do lose, if not for the fact that would just mean that I would have to wait longer to pee," Jill said as she pressed her knees tightly together.

Henry laughed. "That's okay Jill, seeing you aggravated in line like this I feel like I have won already."

"Me too," Dennis said as the three of them laughed.

"Hey I moved up a space finally," Jill said as she stepped forward a few inches.

James came back over. "Well Jill I hate to tell you this but Susan is already 22nd in line while you're 32nd. You're losing Jill!"

"Dammit!" Jill shouted. "And I want to emphasize that I'm not annoyed that you're going to lose, I'm annoyed because she's 10 paces ahead of me in line, what the hell is with that?!"

"I'm not one for statistical analysis but there is the fact that there were more men in her line who were probably going quicker," James said. "And Jill I think that somebody is hogging the porta potty that you are waiting for."

"Freaking figures, this is why I hate individual lines!" Jill shouted. "It should be first come first serve whenever a porta potty opens and just one single line."

"Well Jill that wouldn't be practical," Henry said. "If everyone was waiting in one single line there would just be one long line stretching off into infinity, this is a more efficient use of space."

"And now suddenly you are a statistical analyst," Jill shouted.

"Susan moved up to 19th in line," James said as he came back. "You're still in 31st."

"That's my girl!" Dennis shouted.

"This doesn't have anything to do with skill, it's all luck," Jill said.

"You're just frustrated because you're losing," Dennis said.

"I'm frustrating because my bladder feels like it's ready to explode!" Jill said now unable to avoid grabbing herself and shaking.

"She's definitely in the red zone," Dennis said.

"Definitely," James said.

15 minutes later.

"It looks like we have a winner!" Dennis said as Susan came running back towards them with a smile on her face as he grabbed her and kissed her. "That's my girl!"

"God dammit she didn't do anything, it was purely a matter of chance!" Jill shouted.

"You're just jealous because you lost," Susan said. "I mean wow, your line seems like it's hardly moved at all. How many people does she have in front of her?"

"She still has like 17 in front of her," James said. "You really are unlucky Jill."

"Wow, God damn," Susan said as she laughed.

"Hey show a little compassion for me, you were in my situation not long ago," Jill said as she danced in place barely able to stand still.

"There but for the grace of God go I," Susan said with a laugh.

"I wanna go!" Jill shouted!

"Now she's all pure white and empty," Dennis said as he hugged Susan close to him.

"I have to admit that now that I've won and that I have finally gone to the bathroom I feel pretty amazing," Susan said. "I seriously had to piss, it was a real gusher!"

"Can we chat about something else," Jill said as she stood in line trembling.

"Ha Jill has to pee," Henry said. "I think this is the worst that she's ever had to pee, she is so red that she is practically a supernova."

"Can we please talk about something else?!" Jill said as she pulled her hair.

"We could talk about how you lost the contest to Britney the other day," James said.

"I can't believe I lost to that airhead!" Jill shouted.

"Hey I'm no airhead," Britney said as she came over blowing a bubble with her gum and popping it.

"Britney, what are you doing here?" Jill said.

"Well it really is a small world, I mean what are the odds," Henry said as he laughed.

"Hey I may be an airhead but I think that we all know who the superior bladder is around here," Britney said. "I can hold it all day, so I'm not going to have to use the nasty ass toilets they have here."

"They really are fucking nasty," Susan said. "I certainly wasn't going to sit on those, good thing I know how to hover."

"But you know hovering compounds the problem for women who have to use the toilet after you!" Jill shouted.

"Jill can't hover," James said as everyone began laughing.

"Hey babe what are you doing over here," Mark said as he came over. "Hey isn't that girl you beat in the contest yesterday."

"I like totally kicked her ass," Britney said as she popped her gum once again.

"Is everybody I ever had an awkward bathroom situation with going to just magically show up all the sudden," Jill said.

"Hey you guys from before, you're still waiting in line for the bathroom," Janet said as she came over.

"Nope, just Jill," Henry said. "She still has like 13 people ahead of her in line."

"Unlucky 13," James said.

"Unlucky 13 for unlucky Jill," Dennis said.

"This is a nightmare," Jill said as she continued dancing in line.

"Hey why don't we all take a selfie together?!" Britney said as she took out her phone.

"I don't know, it's kind of awkward to have someone take your picture when you have to go to the bathroom," Jill said.

"Don't be a spoilsport Jill, give it to her as a concession prize to the fact that she beat you in the contest yesterday," James said.

"Fine, but be quick about it!" Jill said as she crossed her legs tightly, bent at the knees and grabbed herself as the women gathered around Jill and the men got behind them and smiled.

"Group selfie!" Britney said as she took the picture and then looked at it. "Jill you totally ruined the picture, can we see a smile next time maybe?"

"I'll smile when I get to pee!" Jill said practically in tears.

"We have to admit that we tried cheating in the contest the other day Britney," Henry said. "We didn't want to say anything but we have awesome psychic powers."

"What are you talking about?" Britney asked.

"We have the psychic ability to know how badly women have to go to the bathroom and we thought that Jill was a shoe in to beat you, but apparently you can just hold it in a lot longer than she can," James said.

"How on earth could you know that?" Britney said. "And don't get too complicated, I'm not an airhead but I'm also not a science person."

"You mean a scientist!" Jill snapped as she stood there bobbing up and down.

"I knew there was a word for that," Britney said as she started giggling.

"It has to involve seeing some type of glowing aura around women that shows how badly they have to go to the bathroom," Dennis said. "I have it as well and I thought that I was the only one."

"Dude is that what that is!" Mark shouted. "I've been seeing weird glowing around women all the time lately as well and I thought that I was suffering from some type of visual problem."

"No you didn't," Jill said.

"Yes I did, right now you're like a blinding red," Mark said.

"That's because Jill is about to explode!" James said as he laughed.

"This is not happening, this is not happening, this is not happening," Jill said as she stuck her fingers in her ears and stomped around.

As Jill stood there ready to explode the rest of the group that was gathered around her as spectators to her desperate agony all continued to exchange stories, making that the count of now four men that she knew who had the psychic ability to know that she was exploding.

"Finally I'm next!" Jill shouted as the woman in front of her got into the bathroom.

10 minutes later.

"Good God what are you doing in there!" Jill shouted as she pounded on the door.

"Hey some things can't be rushed," the woman said as she opened the door. "You might want to wait a minute before going in there."

"I can't wait another minute," Jill said as she opened the door to the porta potty and held her nose. "Jesus Christ. This really isn't my lucky day."

"Glad I don't have to go in there," Britney said as she held her nose and waved her hand in front of her face and started giggling.

Jill closed the door behind her and continued holding her nose. As she looked at the toilet in front of her she saw that it was completely filthy and filled to the brim with all sorts of paper and the seat appeared to be wet.

"I can't use that!" Jill said as her eyes filled with tears as she suddenly felt a spasm in her bladder. "Okay I guess I will have to learn to hover!"

Jill very slowly pulled down her pants and began to make a squatting motion as her thighs trembled. She realized that she was not fully in line with the toilet so she moved her ass over the toilet hoping to position herself in a way that she could pee without urinating all over herself.

"Okay Jill just relax and let it flow," she said as she grabbed the sides of the porta potty and tried to position herself over the toilet, but as she did so she slipped and landed right on her ass on top of the toilet. As soon as she did so her bladder exploded with a powerful hissing stream that she felt certain must have reached the speeds of Mach 1.

At that moment she didn't even care that she was sitting on a filthy toilet, feeling the urine of other women making contact with her ass, or the fact that the porta potty smelled like it was a mortuary. At that moment she was so relieved that she just started crying tears of joy. She used at the last of toilet paper and threw it in the clogged toilet, pulled up her pants and walked out.

"How was it?" James asked.

"It was the most horrible and the most wonderful moment of my life, now let's never speak of it again," Jill said.

Britney began laughing hysterically as everyone started joining in.

"Shut up!" Jill shouted as they continued laughing and would continue laughing all the way home.

11

"I just can't believe it, I can't believe that we found other people who have the power," Henry said. "I mean this is totally amazing, it's wonderful, it's the greatest thing that has ever happened in the history of mankind."

"God dammit why can't I get magical desperation psychic aura powers?!" Jill said as she paced back and forth in frustration. "Come on, there has to be some type of common factor between all of you guys. So Dennis and Mark, you said that you didn't eat anything strange before you noticed the powers?"

Dennis shook his head. "Nope I just woke up one day and suddenly I realized that I could see this weird glowing around all of these women. The night before it was just a normal ordinary day where I felt maybe a little bit lightheaded at the most but then I woke up and I had this strange new amazing power. It took me a while to realize what it was, but going around with Susan all the time, well let's just say that she doesn't have the largest bladder."

"Hey my bladder is not that small," Susan said as she crossed her arms and began blushing.

Dennis laughed. "Well your glowing betrays you, even right now you are definitely at stage green."

"Hey shut up!" Susan shouted. "You know it's kind of a bit rude to discuss the contents of a woman's bladder, that's a very private matter."

"Yes, exactly, what Susan said," Jill said.

"But don't you want the power as well?" Dennis said.

"Of course I want the power, and I'm saying it's not fair that only you guys have the power. I mean if everybody had the power that would be different." Jill shook her head. "But how come I don't have the power?"

"Because you're not a guy," Britney said as she blew a bubble with her gum and popped it.

"Britney," Jill said before pausing as she naturally assumed that Britney was going to say something stupid.

"What?" Britney said as she put her hands on her hips in defiance.

"Actually that's a good point," Jill said. "It seems like all of the people so far who have this power seem to be guys. I mean granted we are only going by a sample group of four people, but it seems like every single person who has gained this ability is of the male gender."

"Us guys are pretty great," James said. "And now we are even greater because we have phenomenal psychic power. I knew it, we are the next stage in human evolution, and we are like the X-Men or maybe the x-ray men since we can see the contents of bladders."

"Wait you don't actually have x-ray vision," Jill said. "You don't see how much is in the bladder, you just see a glowing light around women that indicates how full their bladder is. But you can't actually see the bladder contents themselves."

"Yeah but it's basically the same thing," James said. "All we have to do is look at you to know exactly how desperate you are and how fast your desperation is growing."

"Yeah but we also have to remember the desperation is subjective as some women feel it more than others and some women get desperate more quickly than others, I learned that the hard way," Jill said shaking her head.

"I totally kicked your ass in that contest," Britney said as she popped her gum once again.

"That's my girl," Mark said as he put his arm around Britney who smiled and giggled. "Nobody can beat her in a contest of bladder strength."

"Certainly not Jill," Henry said.

"Or Susan," Dennis said as he laughed.

"Hey," Jill and Susan said in unison as Britney stuck out her tongue and smiled.

"Guys we're not here to discuss bladder strength," Jill said.

"Or lack thereof," Henry said as he rolled his eyes as Britney giggled some more.

"But what we want to find out is how exactly you gained this power and whether there are others like you," Jill said. "Then we can take you to a scientist and they can examine you and hopefully figure out how you gained this power."

"Hey I don't want people dissecting me and taking my eyes," Dennis said. "This is probably a gift from the divine and we certainly don't want to subject it to scientific scrutiny. I don't want to be a lab rat. Besides if people know we have this power they will probably be creeped out by us."

Jill shook her head. "Nobody's going to steal your eyes, although it is kind of creepy that you know something really private like how badly a woman has to go to the bathroom."

"I don't mind my guy knowing how much is in my bladder, because I can hold a very full bladder and I am proud of that," Britney said. "We can't all go running to the bathroom screaming in agony every time our bladder gets a little bit full."

"Do you want to play trivia challenge," Jill said.

"What does that mean?" Britney said as she got up in Jill's face.

"Hey let's not fight," Susan said as she came between Jill and Britney.

"Not all of us are self-conscious about the contents of our bladder," Britney said as she blew another bubble.

"Not all of us are bladder exhibitionists either," Jill said.

"Hey just because I am a stripper doesn't make me a, what was that word you used, an extortionist?" Britney asked. "An abortionist? Because I'm totally pro-life."

"Somehow none of these things are coming as shocking revelations to me," Jill said.

"Cool you're a stripper, where do you work?" Dennis asked.

"Dennis!" Susan shouted.

"I am asking for a friend of mine," Dennis said as he looked from side to side.

"But is that friend named Dennis?" Susan asked.

"Maybe, just because I'm named Dennis doesn't mean I can't have a friend who is also named Dennis."

"But doesn't that get confusing," Britney said. "Like do you both call each other Dennis? What do you do if there are more than two of you together, like in a group? This is all getting extremely complicated for my taste."

Henry began whistling with his fingers. "Okay lets everybody calm down. We all got together here today so that we can discuss this new power and what we are going to do with it."

"I think that maybe we should all form some type of secret superhero team," James said.

"What kind of superhero team can you be just because you can see how badly women have to go to the bathroom?" Jill asked. "As jealous as I am of your power I have to admit that for any practical purposes it's a pretty stupid and ridiculous power. It's not like you can leap tall buildings in a single bound nor have bullets bounce off of you. All you can do is telling that women have to go to the bathroom and how bad. What are you going to go around trying to rescue women from bladder distress?"

"Hey that would be a pretty great idea," Britney said. "Well not for people with amazingly superhuman strong bladders like me, but like little old ladies and people like Jill who can't hold their pee in very long, well you could go around rescuing them from their bladders exploding because bladders exploding could kill people, like all those terrorists in the Middle East who blow their bladders up and splatter all over the people to lose their virginity. Hey I have really great bladder strength, maybe I have superpowers too!"

Super intelligence isn't one of them, Jill thought to herself as she rolled her eyes but she didn't want to say it aloud because then it would start another fight.

"I always kinda wanted to be a superhero," Mark said.

"Hey you've always been a superhero to me," Britney said as she kissed him.

"Aw babe, you're the best," Mark said as he began blushing. "You know what I like that idea, let us form a superhero team where we will go around protecting defenseless women in pee distress."

"Just because a woman has to go to the bathroom doesn't make her a damsel in distress," Jill said shaking her head.

"I don't know you looked like you were pretty much in a lot of distress last night Jill and probably could have used rescuing," Dennis said.

"Yeah I totally beat you in that contest," Susan said.

"I beat Jill in a contest too, we have that in common," Britney said as she high-fived Susan.

"Hey, that last one wasn't even much of a contest, that was just a matter of luck because your line had more guys on it," Jill said as she looked at Susan.

"Jill is just a sore loser," Britney said.

"A sore loser with a sore bladder," Henry said as everyone began laughing. "And really unlucky as well."

"Hey maybe I have superhuman luck," Susan said.

"People just because you can do something that nobody else can do or that you are little bit lucky or that you can hold your pee a long time doesn't mean that you have superpowers," Jill said.

"Jealous!" everyone said.

"Okay fine I can read minds, think of a number between one and 10," Jill said.

"Okay got a number," Britney said.

"Is it seven?" Jill asked.

"No but it was six, you were like super close," Britney said. "Oh my God you actually can read minds!"

"No I was just guessing, I can't read minds," Jill said.

"Oh my God I was just thinking that she couldn't read my mind, she must have read my mind and known that, she's in my head, get out of my head!" Mark said as he grabbed his head and began pacing back and forth.

"God give me strength," Jill said as she rubbed her forehead thinking that she wasn't exactly dealing with a Mensa meeting right now. Finally she whistled. "Okay people let's focus on the specific power of reading auras. Now I have read a lot about psychic phenomenon and I have heard about people being able to read auras to tell that people were feeling sick or what their health was, so maybe it's not a huge stretch to think that some people can suddenly read auras that read how badly a person has to go to the bathroom, or women specifically. Why the power would be that specific I have no idea, but I guess it's not entirely unprecedented."

"Maybe we should go back to the psychic," James said.

"What psychic?" Jill asked.

"James and I went to a psychic trying to figure out how our powers might work," Henry said. "She seemed to think that we were all kind of crazy but we totally were able to predict that she had to go to the bathroom and it was pretty damn funny."

"I once went to a psychic who told me that my grandmother

loved me, how could she have known that?" Britney said.

"Did you tell her your grandmother's name?" Jill asked.

"No but she said my grandmother was watching me and said that she was very proud of me," Britney said with a smile.

"That she was very proud of you for working at the strip club?" Jill asked.

"She didn't say that specifically," Britney said as she scratched her head. "But I mean she didn't say she disapproved of me working at the strip club, I mean I think she was like a flapper or something like that in the 20s, you know 20s era strippers."

"Did the psychic tell you anything that was not extremely general and something that anyone could guess like that a person had a grandmother who died and that their grandmother probably loved them," Jill said.

"Are you saying that my grandmother didn't love me?" Britney said as her eyes filled with tears.

"No I didn't say anything like that at all, don't put words into my mouth," Jill said.

"Because I can call my grandmother and she will tell all of you that she totally loves me," Britney said as she got out her cell phone.

"Wait a minute your grandmother is still alive?" Jill said.

"Well yeah, of course my grandmother is still alive, why should that matter?"

"You said that the psychic contacted your grandmother in the afterlife and your grandmother was still alive. You don't see a problem with this?"

"Stop trying to confuse me!" Britney shouted. "My Granny loves me!"

"You know Jill it's really not nice to tell somebody that their grandmother doesn't love them," Henry said.

"Yeah Jill just because you're jealous that you're not a psychic like us doesn't mean you should be mean," James said. "Besides I thought you believed in psychic phenomenon?"

"Yes I do believe in psychic phenomenon, but psychics who charge you money and tell you very general things I have more of a problem with," Jill said. "I wasn't saying that her grandmother didn't love her, I am just saying that not all psychic readers are legitimate. The fact that she was telling Britney that her grandmother was watching her from the afterlife when she was still alive is kind of a red flag for me that maybe that psychic is not the most legitimate psychic on the planet."

"Wait Granny is watching me?" Britney said. "All the time, like even when I am in the bathroom? That's gross; I'm going to send a really mean text to my grandmother telling her to stop watching me in the bathroom!"

"Wow when she goes to the bathroom it must be pretty epic if she has the bladder strength that you have been telling me about," Susan said. "But then again all she did was beat Jill and even I was able to do that."

"You didn't beat me, you just happened to be lucky enough to have a quicker moving bathroom line," Jill said shaking her head. "Wait a minute I know what we've got to do."

"Right we have to do like Jill suggested, we have to get our ass to the psychic!" Henry said.

Jill was about to say something but everyone was already heading towards the door so she just shrugged her shoulders. "You know what, fuck it, I give up, I am tired and just going to go with this and see what happens."

It didn't take them long to arrive at Madam Melinda's psychic place, or it wouldn't have if the guys didn't stop every couple of minutes to look at a woman that they thought was desperate to pee. She had to admit that she looked as well but she was still thinking that the guys were getting a bit carried away with their new psychic abilities.

"Oh it's you again," Melinda said as she saw Henry and James walk into the shop." Those guys who said that they could read a person's aura to tell how badly they had to go to the bathroom."

"I see you remember us," James said with a laugh. "Sorry last time that we were kind of mean to you and almost made you wet your pants, we were just sort of having fun with you. We hope that you won't take it personally."

"Hey are these one of those dream eater things," Britney said as she picked up a dream catcher. "Because I don't want my brains to be eaten."

"Well there's no risk of that happening," Jill whispered as she rolled her eyes.

"Anyway Melinda we were just hoping that maybe you could give us some insight into our psychic powers," Henry said. "I realize that the nature of our psychic powers is different than the nature of your psychic powers, but we are kind of wondering if you have advice for people who have extraordinary abilities like we do."

"I read people's futures and see deep within their souls," Melinda said shaking her head. "You claim that all you can see is what is in a person's bladder."

James shook his head. "Now Melinda don't get jealous just because we have the more interesting power, we just wanted to talk to a psychic who knows how to handle these types of things. Besides we can tell that you don't have to go to the bathroom right now, at least not that bad anyway."

"I knew that you would come back," Melinda said.

"How did you know that?" Henry asked.

"Oh I know, it's because she's psycho," Britney said with a smile.

"That is psychic Britney, psychic not psycho," Jill said as she shook her head once again.

"If you want to see me go psycho keep annoying me," Melinda said. "But no, I didn't use my psychic powers to ascertain the fact that you would be back, it was just common sense in this case. Since you saw me not long ago I have talked with several other men who all told me the same thing. They said that they were suddenly seeing some type of psychic aura that related to how badly a woman had to go to the bathroom."

"You mean only men have come to you about the ability and no women?" Jill asked.

"That is correct," Melinda said as she nodded. "So far it seems like all the people who have this ability seem to be men and they can exclusively see how badly women have to go to the bathroom. So I am sorry that I dismissed you so easily last time. I guess maybe I was being narrow-minded. But to make it up to you I will tell you something amazing that I saw in the future. I looked into my crystal ball and was able to see the future."

"Wow you have an amazing crystal ball, where can I buy one of those?" Britney asked.

"This is a mystical relic that has been passed down from many generations from my Gypsy grandparents in Europe," Melinda said. "It's not something that you can buy cheaply on the Internet."

"I found it available for as little as $30 on eBay," Jill said as she held up her phone.

Melinda shook her head. "It's not the crystal ball that has the power; it is just a focusing device for the psychic. Do you want to hear what I have seen for the future?"

"Well we came all this way, we might as well," Susan said.

"This is only the beginning," Melinda said. "I believe that we are at the dawn of a new psychic age where powers like this are going to become increasingly common, it could be a new age of enlightenment, or it could be a new dark age, I wasn't quite clear on that. But what I can tell you is that something is coming, something like a tidal wave is going to wash over the world and it's never going to be the same ever again. What was once a trickle will soon become a flood."

"Okay this is just random grandiose predictions now to make everything sound really dramatic," Jill said. "All this talk about floods and trickles and tidal waves, it's just a lot of showmanship and it can get rather annoying."

"Don't mind her, she just doesn't like all of the flood and trickle talk because she has to go to the bathroom," Henry said.

"I don't have to go to the bathroom!" Jill said as she stomped her foot down but they could notice that her leg was shaking a little.

"She has to go to the bathroom," James said.

"Yeah she is glowing bright red right now," Dennis said.

"Jill's gotta pee!" Mark said as he laughed.

"I do not have to pee!" Jill said as she stood there as the room grew silent and she started twitching as everyone stood there staring at her and she was getting uncomfortable. "Well I drank a lot of water and you had us walking all the way around town all day!"

"The bathroom's that way," Melinda said as she pointed to the bathroom door as everyone began laughing.

"I hate you guys," Jill said as she bolted to the bathroom and slammed the door behind her.

12

"I can't believe I'm going around with you guys in public when you are dressed like that," Jill said. "What happened to the idea of keeping this ability secret so that people won't want to dissect you like lab rats and using the power discreetly so that nobody knows about it?"

"We figure it's really cool to be superheroes," Henry said as he pointed to his spandex uniform with a picture of a bladder on it. James, Mark and Dennis were all wearing similar outfits.

Jill shook her head. "First off I don't even really think that the symbol on your chest even really looks like a bladder, it's just not obvious. People are going to look at you and think that you are crazy and that I am crazy for being around you."

"You are kind of crazy Jill," James said.

"Yes, but not going around wearing spandex superhero outfits with a picture of bladder on them level crazy!" Jill shouted.

"She's just totally jealous that she doesn't get to be a superhero with superpowers like we do," Dennis said.

"Guys while I fully admit that I am jealous of you having the superpowers, as you call them, at the same time if I had this power wouldn't be going around in a spandex superhero outfit with a bladder symbol on it," Jill said. "I mean at least partially because it's very difficult to pee in a one-piece spandex outfit like that, did you even consider that when you made these costumes? I think that soon you're going to be the ones getting pretty desperate."

"We have zippers you know," Dennis said as he pointed to a zipper on his spandex outfit. "Besides Jill what would you do with your powers if you had them?"

"I would quietly enjoy the fact that I now had these newfound powers to know when women have to go to the bathroom and how bad, and I would use it the way you guys were using it before you went completely bat shit crazy and decided to make a public spectacle of yourself and draw tons of attention to yourself," Jill said shaking her head.

"Didn't you learn anything from Spiderman?" Henry asked.

"I learned that I would not go around in a spandex uniform with a bladder symbol on it for the third time," Jill said.

"No, with great power comes great responsibility!" James said. "We have this power and we have to use it for the betterment of mankind. You were right when you said that we were just using it for selfish purposes before, we could be using our powers to fight the forces of evil."

"How does knowing how badly women have to pee allow

you to fight the forces of evil?" Jill said. "I think that is a pretty big stretch of the imagination."

"I think that you're getting a stretch of your bladder," Henry said. "You are already at level green."

"You know I think that you have one more additional superpower other than the ability to see how badly women have to go to the bathroom," Jill said.

"What's that?" Henry asked.

"You have a superhuman ability to be really annoying!" Jill said shaking her head. "Once again I would like to state that this has to be the most asinine thing I have ever seen in my life, and that's really saying something."

"I have to admit that I'm kind of with Jill on this one," Susan said. "You guys really do look ridiculous going around in those superhero costumes and I think lots of people are staring at us and taking pictures."

"I'm not embarrassed," Britney said as she hugged Mark. "I'm proud to be the girlfriend of a genuine superhero."

"Yes Britney I think that none of us are surprised by that," Jill said.

"Who wants to take selfies with a superhero?" Britney shouted as she took out her phone and began snapping all sorts of pictures.

"What type of superhero are you?" a woman said as she came up to Mark. "Do you have the ability to leap tall buildings in a single bound or lift something really heavy?"

"No, I am, I'm Bladder Man," Mark said as he flexed his muscles. "I have the superhuman ability of being able to tell how badly women have to go to the bathroom just by looking at them."

"Why is he flexing his muscles, super strength isn't his superpower," Jill said. "In fact his ability to see how badly women have to go to the bathroom also isn't much of a superpower. And yes I am jealous that I don't have it but it's still not really a superhero type of superpower."

"Yeah but he also took the best superhero name," Henry said.

"Yeah I kinda wanted to be Bladder Man," Dennis said.

"It is not the best superhero name!" Jill shouted. "It's just the most obvious name that he thought of off the top of his head and the fact that you guys also thought of the exact same name shows how unoriginal you are."

"What name would you have picked Jill?" James asked.

"I don't know but it wouldn't be Bladder Girl," Jill said as she shook her head.

"Hey everybody I'm Bladder Girl!" Britney shouted from a distance as she waved and put her arm around Mark.

"And that just showed exactly why I would not be Bladder Girl," Jill said.

"What exactly are you are superpowers?" someone said as she came over and looked at James, Henry and Dennis.

"We all have the ability to psychically see how badly a woman has to go to the bathroom," Dennis said.

"You all have the same superpower, that's kind of lame and stupid and also a bit creepy," the woman said before turning to Jill. "Do you have any superpowers?"

"Yes I have super common sense, a power that very few people have," Jill said. "I have the common sense not to dress up like an idiot in public."

"Yeah, but not the common sense to not hang out with people who do," the woman said as all the guys started laughing.

"Burn," Dennis said.

"She was making fun of the three of you or the four of you or probably the five of you since she's actually seen Britney as well," Jill said. "At least Britney had the good sense that you lacked to not dress up in a stupid costume."

"Hey everybody how do I look in the superhero cape that Mark lent me have so that I wouldn't feel left out," Britney said as she came over waving her cape.

"I should have seen that coming," Jill said. "Well anyway I am waiting."

"Waiting for what?" Henry asked.

"Waiting for you to use your powers in some way that's actually useful to the world at large," Jill said.

"We need to go someplace where women are in bladder distress," Dennis said. "I think that I have the perfect idea. Everybody follow me."

Jill had to admit she wasn't exactly sure why she was following her friends around while they were making public spectacles of themselves, but she had to admit it was rather entertaining, and since they knew how badly women had to go to the bathroom it would be interesting to see who they would spot next. As much as Jill thought that they were being idiots, at the same time she couldn't deny that she was still finding their powers to be extremely entertaining, even if she was jealous that she did not have them herself.

Dennis soon led the entire group to a fast food place where they could see that there was a long line to the restroom at the ladies room.

"Okay so you spotted a good line, what are you going to do about it?" Jill said.

"Well I can certainly see that there are women here in urinary distress," Dennis said. "And where there are women in urinary distress there is Bladder Man!"

"Hey I'm Bladder Man!" Mark said.

"Did you call it?" Dennis asked.

"You know for people with superpowers who claim to be superheroes you are both very juvenile," Jill said.

"Jealous," Henry and James said at the same time.

"What we are going to do Jill is that we are going to let the women in line know using our psychic powers who is the most desperate," Dennis said. "Then we can have the women go to the bathroom in the order of how badly they have to go rather than first come first serve."

"But that doesn't seem very fair," Jill said. "Also do you think that the women are actually going to listen to you? I mean if I hadn't seen it with my own eyes I never would have believed that you had magical, supernatural or mutant powers, or whatever you want to call them to know how badly women have to go to the bathroom."

"Well of course they are not going to believe me Jill," Dennis said. "But when I have three friends who also have the same power how can they possibly deny it?"

"I would think pretty easily," Jill said.

"Yeah I had thought she has a point," Susan said. "Maybe this isn't the best idea."

"Nonsense," Dennis said as he walked over to the bathroom line and clapped. "Women of the bathroom line I am appointing myself ladies room line monitor. You may not believe this but I have the psychic ability to know how badly you all have to go to the bathroom, and I think that things would be more efficient if we let the people who had to pee the most go first. I can see that obviously the pregnant woman at the front of the line is literally glowing, she's about to explode, so I am glad that you all saw fit to allow her to cut you in line."

"I've been waiting in line 20 minutes," the pregnant lady said as she danced back and forth. "Not a single person let me cut in line!"

Dennis shook his head. "This is exactly why the world needs superheroes; nobody has common courtesy for a woman in distress. Now I can see that a lot of you woman towards the front of the line don't really have to go to the bathroom that bad. Don't try to deny it, I have psychic powers, you can't hide from me."

"Get out of here you creep!" one woman towards the front of the line said.

Dennis shook his head. "You see she doesn't have to go that bad so she's already getting resentful that I am trying to impose order upon this unruly line of random women."

"And why are you dressed like that?" another woman shouted. "What is that on your shirt?"

"It's a bladder, I'm Bladder Man," Mark said as he stepped forward and pointed to the emblem on his shirt.

The woman in the line all started laughing.

"Haven't you ever heard of Bladder Man," Britney said. "He is here to save women with weak bladders from waiting excessively long in line."

"Who the hell are you?" a woman said as she looked at Britney.

"She's the amazing Bladder Girl," Jill said shaking her head.

"Is this some kind of a joke?" the woman towards the front of the line said.

Dennis shook his head. "It's no joke lady, and I know that you're a lot less desperate than some of the women behind you, so you should do the nice thing, do the right and responsible thing like a superhero would, and let those women cut in front of you in line for the bathroom."

"Hey don't take his word for it, all four of them have superpowers and all of them are equally crazy about it," Jill said as she laughed.

"Don't mind her; she has to pee really badly!" Henry said as he laughed.

"I do not!" Jill shouted but she couldn't deny that by now she did have to go to the bathroom. Walking around with these idiots all day she was trying to avoid the bathroom as much as possible but now nature was finally calling.

"She has a small bladder," Britney said. "Unlike me, who can go all day without going, I know, I won a contest with her."

"Me too," Susan said as she came forward.

"But I thought you thought that this was idiotic too," Jill said to Susan.

"Well I did beat you at that contest Jill," Susan said.

"You just got lucky; it has nothing to do with skill!" Jill shouted.

"Hey what are you doing over here, are you harassing my customers," a man said as he came from the counter.

"We're superheroes," Dennis said. "All we have to do is look at a woman and can tell from the color of glowing around her how badly she has to go to the bathroom."

"What do you mean by the color around her?" the man said. "You know I've been seeing some colors around women lately but I thought I was going crazy."

"Oh come on, not you too!" Jill shouted.

"I think we should talk," Dennis said as he put his arm around the owner of the fast food place.

"Oh good grief," Jill said as she shook her head and palmed her forehead with her hand.

10 minutes later as they started to walk outside of the restaurant.

"Don't worry Harris we will get you a superhero costume soon as well," Dennis said as he put his arm around the fast food store owner and smiled.

"Guys I just have one last thing to say about this whole situation," Jill said.

"What is that?" Dennis asked.

"She has to pee!" everybody shouted.

Jill shook her head and walked back into the fast food place and started walking towards the bathroom. "I don't know why I bother with them, I really really don't."

Although as Jill got on the end of the line she couldn't help but think that it would be nice if some of these women in front of her who didn't have to go as bad would make way for her.

13

What transpired over the next couple of weeks were some of the most dramatic and interesting weeks in the history of the world and Jill found herself glued to every television screen and computer and social media screen that she could find. It really was an exciting time to be alive, but also a very very frustrating one for her particularly.

"And another such incident occurred today when a notable male politician attributed the fact that he won the debate to the fact that he knew that his female opponent had to go to the bathroom extremely bad," the newscaster said. "She found this to be extremely embarrassing to say the least, and these incidents seem to be occurring on a daily basis now that nearly every single man on the face of the planet suddenly has this new ability to read women's desperate need to use the bathroom."

"Quite frankly I think that this is just absolutely humiliating," the woman he was interviewing said. "Women already had enough things to be self-conscious about. We had to worry about our weight, our clothing, our appearance, the way we come across, the way we talk and all these other sexist things that we have to deal with, and now we have to deal with the fact that when we have to go to the bathroom every single man in the vicinity is going to know it. In all honesty I am getting quite sick of it every day."

"And bladder cat calling has become a thing as well," the newscaster said. "Women who need to go to the bathroom find themselves being frequently harassed on the streets by people who know that they have full bladders. It is getting to the point where women either are afraid to go to the bathroom because people will know, or they are afraid not to go to the bathroom frequently because if people know they have to go to the bathroom they will open themselves up to catcalling and harassment. What type of things have people said to you?"

"I was just trying to walk down the block minding my own business," the woman said into the microphone. "And then guys come up to me and they start whistling and hooting and hollering saying look at the bladder on that one, and doesn't she glow so pretty? It's like all the sudden now it seems like a large number of men have developed some type of fetish for seeing women having to go to the bathroom and we can't go anywhere without people harassing us over this fact. Some guy even tried to use a pickup line on me, hey want to come back to my bathroom babe? Want to use me as your own personal toilet? It's making the entire battle of the sexes so much worse."

"And it's not just grown women as well," the newscaster said as he put the microphone up to a little girl who looked sad. "Do the boys tease you when they know you have to go to the bathroom?"

The girl nodded and wiped away a tear.

"And what did the boys say to you?"

"They say can you hold your bladder little girl or they say little Betsy Banner can't control her bladder. And sometimes they call me Betsy Wetsy because sometimes they keep me away from the bathroom and I wet my pants as a result of that."

"And what do you say to them Betsy?"

"My mom said to be like Bruce Banner, the Hulk, she says to tell them you won't like me when my bladder is full."

"Well that's very mature of you Betsy; you have to stand up to bullies, that's what a true superhero does. Thank you for being brave and sharing that with us. Now I think that you probably have to go to the bathroom so I won't keep you."

"Trey that's totally not appropriate," the female newscaster with him said as she shook her head.

"I suppose I would be out of line if I said I know you have to go even worse than she does," he said as he laughed as his co-anchor shot him daggers from her eyes. "And a lot of people have developed what is calling a glow fetish. It used to be when a man told a woman that she was glowing that it meant she was vibrant and looked happy and upbeat and everything like that, but now it has an entirely different meaning. Now when a man tells a woman that she is glowing it means he knows that her bladder is ready to explode. Large numbers of people have developed what is called a glow fetish, where they will get women to hold their bladders as long as possible so that they emit a powerful glow, which many men find extremely attractive. There is even a new phenomenon springing up throughout the country called glow clubs, where men will pay to see women drink until they start glowing from exploding bladders and then bask in the glow. They are probably one of the most asked for services now at strip clubs and many people are trying to line up to cater to and make money off of this mysterious new fetish."

Jill turned off the television. "It's amazing how one seemingly trivial thing can change society in such a profound way through every aspect of society."

"I'm just kind of sad because we're no longer special," Henry said. "Back when we were the only people with this amazing new superpower it was something that made us superheroes, now we are just like every other man on the face of the planet."

"You mean a perverted jerk?" Jill asked.

"No, I mean when I had this it was like a secret between us, we were like a special band of brothers," Henry said.

"Band of bladder brothers," James said with a laugh as he high-fived Henry. "But he's right, now it's almost like we are mortal, no more special than any other guy on the street."

"Well we're still more special than the women I suppose," Henry said. "And I know you're going to say that that is sexist Jill."

"Well the fact that you already know that I'm going to say it should make you aware of your own sexism and how inbuilt it is and how this is making it worse," Jill said. "I almost wish that this had never happened. Sure it was interesting and cool when you were able to see when women had to go to the bathroom, but now that every man is completely obsessed with this new ability it's just growing tedious and annoying constantly hearing about it."

"Jealous!" everyone in the room shouted.

"Well of course I'm jealous!" Jill shouted. "Here's an ability that I would absolutely love to have that 50% of the population has and that I don't have, I think that you would be jealous if it were the other way around."

"Well women still get to be special by giving birth and everything like that," Henry said.

"Oh very special, getting to be pregnant with something inside of you for nine months that is destroying your bladder and then rips your insides out and disfigures your genitals out of alignment for the rest of your life afterwards," Jill said. "I'll be honest I would trade it for the ability to be able to know how badly other women have to go to the bathroom. This is just one more unfair advantage that men now have over women and they are already lording it over us everywhere we go. You guys sure love being special don't you?"

"Hey I still think that I'm pretty special," Britney said as she blew her gum into a bubble and popped it.

"Oh you're definitely special all right Britney, I'm sure lots of people have always been telling you that," Jill said.

"Thank you for finally acknowledging how special and awesome I am," Britney said. "It is not just because I'm really attractive, but the fact is that I have a big big big bladder and a lot of guys find that very attractive."

"Now you're making me jealous," Mark said. "It's crazy that they now have dating websites where you can go to in order to match up with women who have bladder capacities that you would find the most compatible. I never thought I would live in a world where a standard option on dating sites was bladder size preference in women."

"I don't know that kind of makes sense, knowing how often a woman has to go to the bathroom is something you would want to know if you're going to be going everywhere with her," Henry said. "Personally I like it when a woman has to go to the bathroom a lot. It's also useful knowing when a woman really has to go to the bathroom or whether she's faking it."

"Really, now we are discussing faking having to go to the bathroom like we were talking about faking orgasms," Jill said. "I can't believe how fast the world has changed. This has been a real whirlwind for everyone."

"Speaking of having to go to the bathroom we should get to that new multiplex where Dennis got that new job as a bathroom line monitor," James said.

"I honestly can't believe that actually became a thing," Jill said. "Now guys with no other skills suddenly can get a job monitoring a bathroom line and ordering the line around based on the order of how badly the women have to go to the bathroom. Something about that is so fucking ridiculous. But I think that I'm not surprised that this happens at all, ever since the dawn of time men have made a habit of regulating women's bodies in any way possible and I can tell you that we don't really appreciate it."

"I don't know, I think it makes a lot of sense," Britney said. "I mean I would think someone with a small bladder like you would appreciate it Jill. Personally I never have to use public bathrooms or anything like that because my bladder is just so amazing and awesome, but if I had to go to the bathroom really bad and I couldn't wait I would like to be able to cut in line based on how badly I have to go. All I know is that ever since that this change occurred is that I'm getting a lot more attention because of my amazing bladder."

"Who's my little bladder slut," Mark said as he held Britney tight as she giggled and smiled.

"Well come on let's get to the multiplex because Dennis is expecting us," James said as they all got ready.

It didn't take them long to arrive at the new multiplex where you could see lots of women were decidedly uncomfortable about getting those large sodas at the movies because they knew that they would have to go to the bathroom, but by the time the movie was over there was that normal charge towards the bathrooms.

"Okay everybody line up according to need," Dennis said. "It's like the old maxim goes, from each according to their bladder size to each according to the fullness of their bladder."

"Did you just paraphrase Karl Marx in regards to bladder regulation?" Jill asked.

"Well Jill I can see you have to go to the bathroom but there are other women in line who have to go to the bathroom more than you do," Dennis said. "I'm afraid that you will have to let a couple of women cut you."

"You know this isn't really in the spirit of equality," Jill said as she went to where Dennis directed her. "I've always believed in equality of outcome but nitpicking things down to the point where we arrange people according to bladder size and fullness seems like it's just creating another hierarchal class system."

"She's just jealous that she has to go to the back of the line," Susan said as she went towards the front.

"How come she gets to go so far in the front, I think this is nepotism!" Jill shouted. "It's pure bladder size nepotism."

"Hey she just has to go more," Dennis said. "I am completely fair and objective as a bathroom line monitor and I am one of the most experienced bathroom line monitors there is."

"This is just a newly created position that hasn't even existed a couple of weeks yet, stop acting like you are a Nobel laureate for being able to arrange women in a bathroom line!" Jill shouted.

The line was truly gargantuan and the fact that Jill found herself towards the end of the line despite the fact that she had to go to the bathroom relatively badly was rather annoying. As more women joined the line Dennis directed many of them towards the front.

"This is ridiculous, I'm going to be waiting here all day!" Jill said. "This should be first come first serve."

"It is each according to their abilities and needs Jill," Henry said. "Given that you are always into socialism I would think that you would probably have been down with something like this."

"No I think that this is just sort of a stupid use of people's powers to give them jobs," Jill shouted. "One of these days the bladder proletariat is going to rise up against this unfair system that rewards women who waited too long to go to the bathroom by letting them go first. Also it's easy for you guys to talk because there is no freaking line for your bathroom ever! If women had this ability instead of men I guarantee that it wouldn't be a position the other way around. You could get rid of this entire profession by just providing enough bathrooms for women so that everybody can use the bathroom in a timely manner regardless of need."

"Let's not get involved in a deep sociopolitical discussion about the bathroom line Jill," Henry said

"I really have to pee!" the little girl in front of Jill said as a boy came over and began pointing at her and laughing. "Jacinda has to pee, Jacinda has to pee!"

"Hey leave her alone," Jill said.

"What's your problem lady," the boy said. "Oh of course I know your problem, you have to pee even more than she does."

"Why are boys always so much more immature compared to girls," Jill said shaking her head. "So your friend has to go to the bathroom, does that mean you have to be a jerk to her? Why don't you just leave her alone?"

"Why don't you make me?" the boy said as he stuck out his tongue at Jill. "Of course you won't because that would mean getting out of line."

"I'm just more mature than that," Jill said turning her head away from the boy.

"That silly old lady has to pee!" the boy said as he danced and pointed at Jill." She has to pee, she has to pee!"

"Oh shut up already!" Jill said as she stuck out her tongue as the boy stuck his tongue out at her. "And I'm not an old lady, I am in college!"

"What are you studying, urology?" the boy said as he burst out laughing. "Of course not because boys are better urologists because they always know how bad you have to go to the bathroom. Girls can't be urologists."

"We can too!" Jacinda shouted.

"You tell him girl!" Jill said as she patted Jacinda on the shoulder as she continued dancing and pacing in line looking uncomfortable.

"What's going on?" James asked.

"Jill is getting in an argument with a young boy about the sociology of the bathroom and I think that he is probably kicking her ass," Henry said.

"Hey everybody what's going on," Mark said as he came over with Britney on his arm smiling and blowing her gum.

"Jill thinks that she's a genius," Britney said.

"Well genius is on a sliding scale and it's all a matter of comparison," Jill said. "I know certainly compared to some people I pretty much am a Nobel laureate."

"Hey I think I was one of those ones," Britney said. "But I know that I am a bladder laureate because I can out hold anyone!"

"I love this new bathroom line system," Susan said as she came out of the front of the bathroom. "It got me a fast track to the front of the line because I got desperate more quickly than others."

"This honestly hardly seems fair," Jill said shaking her head as she danced in place as Dennis motioned more women towards the front of the line while Jill and Jacinda lagged far behind.

The little boy kept dancing around the line pointing and laughing at Jill as she just tried to ignore it until it was finally her turn to go to the bathroom. But just as she was getting towards the front of the bathroom more people came out from another movie theater and were ushered in front of her.

When Jill finally came out of the bathroom with Jacinda the little boy who was laughing suddenly frowned and began running away.

"You see Jacinda you can always count on one thing, the biggest bullies are always the biggest cowards," Jill said. "Don't ever let that guy bother you again, can you promise me that?"

"Yes I can," Jacinda said as she nodded and ran off.

"Way to quote Obama," Jill said as she put her fist up in the air doing a solidarity power fist. "So where are we all going to go now?"

"Drinks!" everybody shouted as they began laughing.

Jill rolled her eyes and laughed as well as she shrugged her shoulders. "You know I should have seen that coming."

14

Jill had to admit that it was nice that while female pee desperation was now a mainstream topic of discussion throughout the world she was getting kind of sick of hearing about it. She always thought it would be a good thing if people were more open about their bodily functions, particularly women, but now that everything was out on display it was getting to be too much and most people were less than mature about it.

"I never thought I would see the day when you didn't like hearing about women desperate to pee Jill," Henry said as they were walking to class.

"Look I admit that I was jealous of your ability and I thought that it was cool when it first happened, but I think that you have a good point as well, it's no longer very special," Jill said. "Now that everybody knows how badly all women have to go to the bathroom all the time it's not quite as fun."

"Not all people just having to go to the bathroom, it's only men who know when women have to go to the bathroom," James said.

"Well yes that's partially the reason why it's so annoying and frustrating," Jill said. "It's just that guys already had so many advantages over women and now that they know when we have to go to the bathroom it's like they have one upped us once again. It was one thing when we were just looking at women and wondering if they were desperate, but now that you can tell just by looking at them without them showing any signs it just seems really intrusive."

"I can kind of understand that," Henry said. "Now this whole thing has become sort of a national debate as if it's rude or something to ask women their bladder size, not that we even need to ask because now it's blatantly obvious to anyone looking how fast a woman has to go to the bathroom and how long she can hold it."

"And now people are probably going to use that as a way of discriminating," Jill said. "And think of all the privacy concerns that it brings up. Be honest, if the situation were reversed and every woman that you came across knew how badly you had to go to the bathroom wouldn't you feel a little bit self-conscious, even just a little bit? Wouldn't you find it sort of intrusive to your privacy for people to know when you had to go to the bathroom all the time and that you couldn't conceal it from them?"

"I suppose that could be rather annoying," Henry said. "And while I fully understand all of your concerns Jill at the same time I am still happy to have this newfound ability, even if it's no longer all that special. The fact is you just can't put the genie back in the bottle. This is just the world that we live in now, we now live in a world where all men have the ability to know when women have to go to the bathroom and that's all there is to it. You're just going to have to learn to live with it."

"I could live with it a lot easier if I had the ability as well," Jill said. "If women knew how badly everyone had to go to the bathroom at least we would be on equal playing field."

"Yeah but if women knew how badly each other had to go to the bathroom there would be all sorts of cat fights in lines for the bathroom," James said.

"Well unlike guys women are little bit more civilized," Jill said. "We wait patiently in those long lines as you guys walk in and out of the bathroom without any wait, and now you even have women waiting patiently while someone else directs us in line. I have to say that bathroom line monitor is the new Walmart greeter of this generation. I can't really picture a stupider and more unnecessary job."

"I don't know it's kind of a useful thing, don't you think?" Henry said. "It's almost like lanes in a supermarket. You have the 10 items or less line for people who don't have as much that they need to ring up so they don't have to wait as long. Now you have a system where the people who have to go to the bathroom get to go right away and the people who can wait longer can wait longer."

"But don't you see how unfair that is?" Jill said shaking her head. "It means that unless you get in line when you are already bursting to pee you could end up waiting an exceedingly long amount of time as people go in front of you. It's just totally not fair at all. It's like it rewards you for waiting until the last minute and I just don't think that that's very fair or very right at all. And it's affecting people's behavior as well."

"Affecting people's behavior how?" James asked.

"Well now a lot of women are waiting until the last minute to go to the bathroom so that they can get to the front of the line, meaning that lots of desperate women all go towards the bathroom at once. And then there are certain other women who don't even bother getting in line unless they're ready to explode. But there are some who do the total opposite and may keep going to the bathroom as much as possible so that they won't be glowing very much and draw unwanted attention to themselves."

"Well for what it's worth we can see that you're not glowing right now," Henry said.

"Of course because we have a big three hour class ahead of us, so I made sure to go to the bathroom beforehand and I am trying to limit how much I drink because I don't want to be lighting up like a searchlight while I am in the classroom."

"I have to admit that those lectures by Mr. Pavarotti really are bladder busters," James said. "And it is hard to pay attention in class, what with all of the glowing women all around."

Jill shook her head. "Hey it's not our fault that we are glowing in class. Just like the same if we wear sexy clothing, it doesn't mean that that gives you the right to harass us or to complain that we are distracting you. If you had control of yourselves you would be able to pay attention regardless of what women are wearing and how much they are glowing. And I can't believe that that is something that I am now saying. Now all the sudden women are glowing all the time and yet we can't even see it ourselves. I have to admit it still is very frustrating."

"Well let's hurry and get to class as we don't want to be late again," James said as he walked into the class to see that most of the women weren't yet at the desperation level, but he could see that several had a faint glow around them.

The three of them took their seats as Mr. Pavarotti began giving his spirited lecture on evolutionary biology. However Jill could notice that Henry and James had their eyes wandering in all directions and she couldn't help but notice that they were looking at one girl in the front row who looked like she had her legs crossed very subtly. If Jill had not been watching them watching her she probably wouldn't have even noticed, but now that she saw that the girl was squirming in her seat she couldn't take her eyes off of her.

"Is something the matter gentleman?" Mr. Pavarotti said as he saw one guy staring at the girl in the front row just like Henry and James had been doing.

"Yeah Mr. Pavarotti the girl who is glowing bright red in the front row is distracting me," said Nelson, one of the guys in the middle of the classroom.

The girl's name was Nicole and she looked and turned at Nelson. "It's not my fault I have to pee! Stop staring at me!"

"Nicole do you need to use the restroom?" Mr. Pavarotti said.

"I think that you know she does, or are you disabled in some way," Nelson said.

"Nicole I think that maybe you should go relieve yourselves as you are obviously being a distraction to the boys in the back row," Mr. Pavarotti said.

"How is that my fault?!" Nicole said as she stood up blushing and walked out of the room as Jill elbowed Henry and James in the side, seeing as Nicole just made the point that she was making a few moments ago.

"Let us everyone try to focus on the lesson and not on the glowing of the women in the classroom," Mr. Pavarotti said. "I have to admit that I often wonder what Mr. Charles Darwin would have said if he had lived to see this evolutionary development in the human race. According to the theory of evolution when a mutation is beneficial for the species it is passed down, however this is a new phenomenon that cannot be explained through conventional evolutionary biology, as I have written in my own thesis paper. Some people want to use the supernatural to explain this mysterious new ability to 'read auras' as some will call it. I still think that there is probably some type of reasonable scientific explanation for why this is happening, even though suddenly gaining an ability like this overnight is evolutionarily unprecedented."

Nelson raised his hand and Mr. Pavarotti pointed to him. "I think I know why it's happening Mr. Nelson. I think it's happening because it's very entertaining!"

Lots of the guys in the classroom began cheering and hooting and hollering and laughing loudly but most of the girls looked decidedly uncomfortable.

"I think that I might know a reason why Mr. Pavarotti," said Charles, another one of the students. "Maybe it is so that we can hunt better."

Jill once again elbowed Henry and James because that was a point that she had made before when she felt like they were stalking that woman at the carnival.

"That makes you sound like a predator," said Jessica a girl in the middle of the classroom. "You're hunting us while our bladders are full, what type of crazy fucked up shit is that?!"

"Okay class calm down," Mr. Pavarotti said as he motioned for everybody to sit down. "It is true that this could be an adaption to hunting in some way, not necessarily in a creepy stalker type of way, but as a way of men assessing women. Women who have greater bladder capacity and to glow more might be more attractive to prospective mates."

"Mr. Pavarotti you sound like a sexist tool of the patriarchal establishment," Jessica said.

"Well anyway let us get back to the lecture on more conventional theories of evolutionary biology that don't involve the full bladders of women," Mr. Pavarotti said as numerous people in the classroom laughed.

As the lecture went on it seemed like Mr. Pavarotti went on and on for hours and by the end of the class the classroom was practically lit up. By then you could see that very few of the guys were paying attention and you could see that many of the women were looking increasingly uncomfortable and self-conscious.

"Well we still have some time left but I think that maybe we can leave early today because I think that a lot of you guys are getting distracted by the glowing of the women, and that glowing indicates that a lot of you women need bathroom breaks, so ladies and gentlemen, you are dismissed," Mr. Pavarotti said as everyone started storming out of the classroom.

"It looks like you're all in the red zone," James said as Jill barreled past him towards the bathroom only to be confronted with the inevitable line.

"See this is what happens when women don't want to get up to go to the bathroom and make things obvious," Jill said as she pointed to the line.

"I think that Jill has made a good point," Henry said. "I can see that most of the women in this line are orange or in the red."

"Hey don't stare," Jessica said from the front of the line.

"I think that we had better get going before these women get all angry and tear us apart, we will meet you in the courtyard Jill," James said as he and Henry walked off.

"The nerve of some guys," Jessica said shaking her head as Jill nodded in agreement. But she had to admit the whole time she was waiting in line she was picturing all of those other women and how they must appear to Henry and James, and every other man in the world, glowing brightly and announcing their need to go to the bathroom to the entire world. And she felt like she was betraying her fellow sisters for the fact that if only she had had the ability herself she would be beyond thrilled, even if she wasn't the only one with that ability.

Once Jill had gotten out of line for the bathroom, which fortunately didn't have a bathroom line monitor because she guessed the college thought that it was a waste of money, which she felt spoke well to the fact that it really is an institute of higher learning, she met up with Henry and James in the college courtyard.

"Damn Jill what took you so long," Henry said with a laugh. "You see that's exactly why you could use a bathroom line monitor in more places."

"Shut up you guys," Jill said. "So what is this place that you wanted to take me to?"

"We wanted to show you where Britney's new job is," James said.

"Somebody hired Britney for a job?" Jill said shaking her head. "What is it a job where she chews gum to test the flavor out? Because I am thinking that that might be a little bit beyond her, I mean walking and chewing gum at the same time, let's not over exert her mentally."

"No she's working at this new place that I think you will find really interesting Jill," Henry said. "But I think that it would be better if it were a surprise."

"You know every time you guys say that you have a surprise it often turns into something regretful," Jill said.

"No trust me Jill, you will find this place interesting," James said as they began walking down the street and Jill couldn't help but notice that not just Henry and James but lots of other guys seemed to be checking out the women in a distinctive way, not for their breasts or ass, but in a new way.

"You know Jill a lot of people are developing a glowing fetish," Henry said. "And I think that we all know that is just a front for the fact that they are too embarrassed to admit that they like seeing women having to go to the bathroom."

"Actually I have to admit that aside from just the fact that knowing they have to go to the bathroom the glow can actually be pretty sexy in a lot of ways," James said.

"Wait a minute, don't tell me Britney doesn't work at a –" Jill started saying as they all stood still in front of the door which said Glow Flow.

"Yep Britney is working at a glow club," James said.

"I feel kind of weird going into a club like this," Jill said as they walked into the door. "The fact that I'm interested enough to go in one, well doesn't it kind of announce to the world that I'm a lesbian?"

"Not necessarily, I mean most lesbians probably wouldn't find a place like this interesting since you can't even see the glow," Henry said.

"I guess that's a pretty good point," Jill said as she looked around to see lots of women standing on stage, many of them being very still, but she knew that all of them must have to go to the bathroom really bad. Once again though she felt disappointed that she couldn't really enjoy watching them glow, and maybe it would be kind of interesting seeing women glowing even if it weren't just for the fact that they had to go to the bathroom. Jill also noticed that the lighting was very low in the room.

"You know I never thought of it like this but do we girls glow-in-the-dark now?" Jill asked.

"You're like living glow sticks," James said with a laugh. "Well not you specifically now as you aren't bursting yet, but look at Britney over there!"

Jill looked over to see Britney on stage in a scantily clad

outfit that looked really tight and formfitting and she couldn't help but notice that even Britney seemed to be shifting a little bit from leg to leg.

"Hey guys you made it," Mark said as he waved them over. "You finally brought Jill to see Britney in action."

"Hi Jill," Britney shouted as she waved while crossing her legs. Jill had to admit it was nice to see Britney in urinary distress if for no other reason than she knew that she couldn't leave the stage.

"Hey Britney, congratulations on becoming a bladder bimbo," Jill said.

"Hey this is hard work," Britney said as she danced from leg to leg. "I bet you couldn't stand up here all day with a bursting full bladder!"

"So you actually have to go to the bathroom," Jill said. "I thought that you never had to go to the bathroom. I have to admit it is somewhat satisfying seeing you actually having to go to the bathroom."

"A lot of guys buy me drinks," Britney said. "A real real real lot of drinks that are a strain even on my comparatively enormous bladder."

"Well hell I'll buy you a drink," Jill said as she bought Britney over a tall glass of alcohol. "Drink up!"

Jill watched with satisfaction as Britney chugged down the beer and appeared to be barely able to stand still.

"What's the matter Britney, can't take all the pressure," Jill said. "Is your glow approaching a flow?"

"Shut up Jill!" Britney shouted as she twisted and contorted her body in ways that Jill didn't even think was humanly possible. "When is my break?!" Britney eventually shouted.

"Hey you don't go off duty until another half hour," the manager shouted back.

"This is going to be a very entertaining half hour," Jill said as she put her feet up and watched Britney dance. Even though she couldn't see Britney glowing, she could see that a lot of other guys were rubbing their eyes looking at her and Jill felt almost a little bit jealous for all the attention that Britney was getting, despite the fact that she didn't really want any attention from guys. The fact that Britney just seemed to be an attention whore who commanded everybody's attention whenever she entered a room was only made worse by the fact that now when she entered a room she literally lit up the entire room.

"I think that this firecracker is about to burst," Henry said as he noticed Jill starting to get up. "Where are you going Jill?"

"Britney is about to get off of her shift, so I feel it is my moral obligation to clog up the bathroom," Jill said as she walked to the ladies room with a smile on her face. When she came out Britney was standing there wet in a leotard.

"Bathroom hog," Britney said as she walked into the ladies room to get changed.

"That was for beating me in the contest," Jill whispered as she laughed.

When Britney came out of the bathroom and all of them were walking home together that night Jill was smiling and grinning from ear to ear.

"What are you so happy about?" Britney, now dressed in more conventional and less scantily clad clothing, said as she blew a bubble with her gum and popped it.

"Nothing I just think this is a very good job that caters to your talents," Jill said. "I really think you found your calling in life."

"Well thank you for finally acknowledging my extraordinary talent," Britney said with a smile not realizing that Jill had actually insulted her by implying that standing on stage until she wet herself was probably the best thing she could hope for in life, at least as far as her skill set went.

"That's my girl," Mark said as he grabbed Britney and pulled her tight. "That's my bladder girl!"

"And you're my bladder man," Britney said as she kissed Mark.

"You know what guys thanks for making me come to the glow club, I think that I really enjoyed it," Jill said.

"We knew you would," Henry said.

"But you didn't even get to see me glow!" Britney shouted.

"No, but although I may not have been able to see the light, I sure saw you shine," Jill said as she put her arm around Britney. "And you know what; I think that that just made my day."

And as Jill walked down the street that night she had to admit that for the first time in a while she found seeing a woman desperate to pee fun again and that was something that had been worth waiting for.

15

Jill's alarm clock woke her up bright and early that morning because that was the day of the big summer festival, an event that every year she looked forward to because there were always good opportunities to see lots of desperation, and she felt sure that the turnout would be especially large this year because many people would probably want to go to see all of the women glowing.

"You don't even care that there is likely to be extremely long lines to the bathroom for you Jill," Henry said as they waited for the bus to arrive.

Jill shook her head. "You know what I've had a couple of weeks to get used to this now and I am not going to let the fact that I don't have a special psychic power diminish my enjoyment of seeing other women desperate to pee, even if it means I'm going to be ending up desperate myself and that it will be obvious to everybody."

"I'm glad that you are no longer self-conscious Jill," James said. "Not that it matters because I can see right now that you don't have to go to the bathroom."

"Well obviously before leaving I'm going to go to the bathroom," Jill said. "By now you should know that about me. But I am looking forward to this, more so this year than in other years. I mean it's always nice to go to the big summer festival to celebrate the end of the school year and the beginning of the summer break, but I am sure that it will be especially popular this year simply because it's going to be late into the night and you're going to get to see all of the women glowing. I'm still super jealous though that I don't get to see the glowing. It must be kind of weird seeing all the women glowing all the time."

"Well you get used to it pretty fast," Henry said.

"Well of course you guys do, you had an interest in this before it was even mainstream, no pun intended," Jill said.

"Pun?" James asked." Oh, mainstream, as in urine stream!" James began laughing.

As they got on the bus Henry and James of course picked the seats next to the women who had to go to the bathroom most. Jill didn't even have to ask if they were doing that as she just intuitively knew at this point. They did it purely out of habit.

"You guys aren't even really disguising it anymore are you," Jill said.

"Why should we," James said. "Everybody knows that every guy has this ability so it's not like we could even turn it off if we want to, not that we want to."

"You still don't think that maybe some women feel weird about the fact that you are sitting next to them just because they are glowing the most," Jill asked.

"Hey it's not a crime," Henry said as he smiled and laughed.

Jill had to admit that she was enjoying watching the women in front of her shifting around in their seats. It was going to be at least an hour bus ride to get to the festival and she knew that by then they would probably be going out of their minds.

"Red alert," Henry whispered to James and Jill.

Jill shook her head. "Looking for reds has an entirely different meaning than it did in the 1950s. Imagine how people from the 1950s would have reacted to something like this!"

"Probably nobody would have talked about it," James said.

"But people would have to talk about it eventually if it was this obvious," Jill said. "But people with the sensibilities of the 1950s would probably find this extremely awkward. Honestly it's pretty awkward right now but imagine people from the 1950s and how uptight they were talking about bodily functions. Imagine if something like this had happened back then, I'm kind of wondering if we would have made more progress as a society or less."

"I'm guessing it would be a mixed bag," Henry said.

"Well at least all of this is making people more aware of women needing to use the bathroom and the fact that women actually do go to the bathroom," Jill said. "I would honestly rather everyone not know exactly how badly I had to go to the bathroom at every given moment, but at least people are now being more open about these issues, so I guess it's all worth it. I still wish I had the ability though."

"Well wish on a shooting star," James said. "We still don't know what caused all of this, so maybe it was something crazy like someone wishing on a shooting star."

"But that sounds rather silly," Jill said.

"Well hey crazier things have happened," Henry said as she

shrugged his shoulders. "I mean maybe it is kind of silly but it can't hurt right?"

Jill shrugged her shoulders. "I suppose you have a point there."

It didn't take them long to arrive at the festival but by the time they did the women in front of them were practically jogging to the front of the bus and Henry and James couldn't help but snicker. Jill just rolled her eyes as she couldn't deny that she was enjoying this as well but she didn't want to be as obviously perverse about it as they were. And since women didn't have the ability to see the glowing she could be much more nonchalant about it because those women wouldn't necessarily know that she knew that they had to go to the bathroom.

As they got off of the bus they quickly met up with Mark, Britney and Susan.

"Hey where is Dennis?" Jill asked.

"Didn't you hear, he got a job at the festival as a bathroom line monitor," Mark said.

"Seriously, they hired bathroom line monitors for the festival?" Jill said shaking her head. "I guess they really did go all out this year didn't they? I was assuming that we would have unisex bathrooms at this place but hopefully not those gross ass porta potties like at that other place."

"I still can't believe you sat on that," Britney said as she giggled and popped her gum.

"Well hey at least I didn't wet my pants," Jill said as she and Britney stuck out tongues at each other.

Jill had to admit that by now she was probably at stage yellow approaching stage blue but she wasn't going to go running to the bathroom just yet. She wasn't going to wait until the last minute of course, but she didn't want to go running off to the bathroom like a crazed fanatic. She figured with so many women at the festival she could probably blend in more easily but she couldn't help but notice that all throughout the festival that guys were looking around and checking out the women more than they used to, and not just the most attractive women.

"I bet all of these guys are checking me out and they are in awe of my massive bladder strength," Britney said.

"Well too bad because you are all mine," Mark said as he pulled Britney close as she giggled and smiled. "You probably won't have to pee at all during the entire festival as you are barely at yellow. Jill is already at blue and Susan I can see that you are getting pretty close to green."

Susan blushed. "Thanks for telling the entire world."

"Come on we didn't come here to discuss our bladders, we came here to look at the bladders of other people," Jill said.

As they all started walking around the place they saw all sorts of different women running to and fro looking for a place to go to the bathroom. Women seemed to be growing less self-conscious about their bladders now that people had begun getting used to it but still a lot of people would run and hide the fact that they were glowing.

"Hey baby, shake that bladder!" Dennis shouted as Susan came over.

"Hi Dennis," Susan said as she went over to him and kissed him. "Have you finally got some time off from your rigorous job as a bathroom line monitor?"

Jill shook her head. "I still can't believe that is an actual job now."

"But it's a pretty good job," Dennis said. "I mean it doesn't really pay all that much but the fringe benefits are worth it. I get to see so many women glowingly desperate for the bathroom all day long."

"Yeah but don't you feel weird about having that as a job?" Jill asked. "Isn't it almost like a really perverted version of being a Walmart greeter?"

"Are you saying that you wouldn't want this job?" Dennis said as he smiled and laughed.

"Look I like seeing women desperate to go to the bathroom but making a career out of it seems like, I don't know, it feels like you should shoot higher," Jill said shaking her head. "I don't know I guess I just set higher expectations for myself than watching people glow and then assigning them a place in the bathroom line based on that."

Dennis shook his head. "Look some men aspire to be doctors, some men aspire to be president, I'm happy with my station in life as a bathroom line monitor. In a lot of ways I am like a pioneer seeing as this job didn't even exist not that long ago."

"Okay let's not get carried away, if you were going to be the first man on Mars I would say you are a pioneer, assigning women places in a line for the bathroom isn't quite the same as landing on Mars," Jill said.

"I still kind of liked it when we thought that we were superheroes," Mark said. "But now that everybody can do it, well it doesn't seem as special."

Henry nodded. "I agree, I miss it when we were superheroes."

"I still have superhuman bladder strength," Britney said as she put her hands on her hips and looked up to the sky like she was about to just start flying away like Supergirl.

"And I can totally read minds," Jill said rolling her eyes.

"What number am I thinking of?" Britney asked as she closed her eyes and put her fingers to her temples.

"Seven," Jill said.

"Oh my God you really can read minds!" Britney said. "What does my grandmother say?"

"She said not to be so gullible," Jill said as everyone began laughing. "Or at least that's what I think she would say if I, you know called her on the phone, because she is still alive."

"And for that I am pretty happy," Britney said as she smiled.

"Although we have to admit that psychic lady was definitely right that time," Henry said. "She said that a new age of enlightenment was coming and that the psychic power was going to wash over the world and all of that stuff."

"But she also said it could be a new dark age," Jill said.

"True but let's try to remain optimistic," Henry said. "I highly doubt that this newfound ability is going to destroy human civilization."

Jill shook her head. "You know what never underestimate human craziness. I have to admit though that for all intents and purposes this could have been a lot crazier. I mean when you consider everything that has happened I suppose the human race has taken it relatively well. Sure there is lots of crazy stuff going on but I guess society hasn't changed all that much, or at least not as much as it could have. And sure people aren't being super mature about it but you are right that being able to know when women have to go to the bathroom isn't going to bring about a new paradigm shift in human history."

"It's the age of Aquarius!" Britney shouted.

"I thought you were a Pisces?" Mark asked.

"I think I was born on the cusp or something like that," Britney said as she smiled and blew her gum.

"You were born on something all right," Jill said as she rolled her eyes. "Anyway do you guys see any new interesting glowing women right now?"

"Well you ladies are all starting to glow," Mark said. "But look at that woman over there, I can't seem to read her." Mark started pointing at a woman who looked like something was agitating her.

"Hey I can't read her either," James said. "How about you guys?"

Henry and Dennis shook their heads.

"What do you mean you can't read her, she's not glowing?" Jill asked. "How is that possible?"

"I have no idea," Dennis said. "Maybe if we follow her around though we will figure it out, she does look like she might need to go to the bathroom."

"But I still feel weird about stalking people like this," Jill said. "But you are right she does look like she is desperate to go."

"She's not the only one," Henry said as Jill realized that her bladder was getting rather full.

"Hey shut up," Jill said as they began following the mysterious woman.

"She is still not glowing," Henry said as they continued watching her but noticed that she seemed like she was shifting from leg to leg. "But she obviously has to go to the bathroom. This really is baffling."

"Oh shit she's coming over here," James said.

"Excuse me," the woman said as she came over. "I couldn't help but notice that you seem to be following me."

"We weren't following you," James said as he looked at his friends but it was pretty obvious that he was lying.

"Don't lie to me," the woman said as she put her hands defiantly on her hips.

"Okay I have to admit we were following you," Henry said. "We didn't mean to be creepy or anything like that, it's just that we can't seem to read you."

"What do you mean read me?" the woman asked. "Wait did you figure it out? And I thought I was passing so well!"

"What do you mean passing?" Jill asked.

"I'm transgender," the woman said. "I was born biologically male but I transitioned and I thought that I passed really well but now I am feeling really self-conscious."

"That's not what we meant at all!" Henry said. "When we said that we couldn't read you we meant that we couldn't see you glowing. Wait a minute, now it all makes sense."

"What makes sense, I don't get it," Britney said as she popped her gum again.

Jill was about to mention that she didn't understand quite what she meant either but she didn't want to sound like she was as stupid as Britney, so she kept her mouth shut.

"I think I get what he means," James said. "Even if she transitioned from male to female as far as her chromosomes are concerned she is still chromosomally male, which means that she wouldn't give off a glow."

"That's right," the woman said.

"Wait a minute, does that mean you also can see the glow on others?" Jill asked.

"Well I can definitely see that you are green with envy and approaching an orange alert," the woman said. "And the woman who keeps popping her gum seems like she is also pretty full."

"Oh my God, she is psychic!" Britney shouted as she popped her gum on her face and began peeling it off.

"She's right," Jill said. "Look we didn't mean to be stalking your anything, we were just kind of curious and wondering why you weren't glowing. We didn't mean anything creepy by it. I'm Jill by the way, that's Britney, Susan, Dennis, Mark, Henry and James." Jill pointed to her friends as she named them.

"My name is Brenda, formally Brandon," the woman said as she shook Jill's hand.

"Well Jill it looks like you found a new person to be jealous of," James said. "Now you found another woman who has the ability to see how desperate other women are. That must be pretty awesome."

Brenda smiled. "It actually is because I can read other

women but no one can read me, so no one knows how badly I have to go to the bathroom." As she said that she crossed her legs.

"I may not be psychic but I can tell that you definitely have to go to the bathroom pretty bad," Jill said as the two of them laughed.

"That is definitely true," Brenda said as she crossed and uncrossed her legs. "I think the one thing I miss about being a guy is the fact that it was much easier to go to the bathroom and I could hold a lot longer. Now it seems like I have to pee all the time and everywhere I go there are lines."

"Amen sister," Jill said as she patted Brenda on the shoulder. "That's how you know you are fully a woman, you will never be able to again pee easily or quickly, never again know what it's like to have male urinary privilege. It must be a loss that you feel deeply every day."

"Guys I think we should all be getting to the bathrooms right now," Susan said. "Dennis maybe you can help us cut in line?"

"But wouldn't that be nepotism?" Dennis asked. "I wouldn't want to abuse my power to show special favors to my friends."

"Yes you would dammit!" Jill shouted as everyone began laughing.

Their entire group started going towards the bathrooms but when they arrived at the bathrooms they saw no lines.

"Oh good there's no line!" Jill shouted. "It's a miracle."

"Well where is the fun in that," Henry said as he crossed his arms and shook his head.

Jill went to the door of the ladies room and found it locked as she pulled on it. "Hey open up!"

"Times like these are the only times I miss my penis," Brenda said as she stood there with her legs crossed right next to Susan who did likewise. The only one standing there casually was Britney who continued blowing her gum and popping it.

"I bet you girls wish that you had superpowers like I have," Britney said as she pointed to herself. "I'm Bladder Girl!"

"How could they lock the bathrooms at an event like this?!" Jill shouted.

"Wow Jill you look red in the face, not to mention red glowing," James said.

"We need the bathroom!" Susan said as she crossed her legs.

"I guess you girls will just have to hold it," Dennis said as he began laughing but the women all just stared at him shooting him daggers, except for Britney who stood there casually popping her gum. "Look as a bathroom line monitor I am sure that they are just closing the bathroom temporarily for cleaning or something like that. I'm sure if you come back in a few minutes or in a half-hour or something like that the bathroom will be open once again."

Susan, Jill and Brenda all grabbed themselves and began moaning in aggravation.

"Now things have really gotten interesting!" Mark said as he started laughing. "But I think that they're going to begin the big concert and fireworks show, so I think that we should try to go get some good seats. We don't want to miss that now do we?"

All of the girls let out aggravated groans, again except for Britney who was still casually popping her gum, as they all slinked off to find seats. They actually managed to get relatively good seats towards the front and they could see that it was starting to get late because now it was distinctly dark out.

"Welcome ladies and gentlemen," the announcer said as he came out on the stage. "Are you ready to see fireworks?"

People in the audience began shouting but you could see that most of the women looked decidedly uncomfortable.

"I can see that a lot of you have a healthy glow out there," the announcer said amid laughter and groans. "Come on ladies stand up and take a bow; let your glow shine for everyone to see!"

Most of the women remained seated but a few of them started slowly getting up like Britney who started blowing kisses to everybody.

"Come on now ladies, don't be shy," the announcer said.

Several more women started standing up and now the guys could see that the place was glowing brightly. Reluctantly Jill, Susan and Brenda all stood up as well, although Brenda knew that she probably stood out by virtue of the fact that she wasn't glowing.

"There we go everybody," the announcer said. "I have to admit that we kind of planned this. You may have noticed that we closed the bathrooms a while ago or at least the ladies rooms anyway. This was going to be our first annual glow festival!"

"Glow festival?" Jill said as she looked at Susan and Brenda.

"Hey I am glowing!" Britney said as she started taking a bow.

The announcer began laughing. "We have to admit it was kind of evil of us but we decided that we would lock all of the ladies rooms a few hours before it got dark so that all you ladies would be lighting up the place during the fireworks show."

"Awesome," Dennis said.

"Did you know about this?" Susan said as she looked angrily at Dennis who simply shrugged his shoulders and smiled.

"Hey a bathroom line monitor's job comes with some degree of secrecy," Dennis said as he laughed.

Several of the women in the audience began shouting and booing at the announcer.

"Now ladies don't get your bladders in a knot, it was all in good fun," the announcer said as people continued booing and shouting and some people began throwing stuff at him. "You have to appreciate some degree of showmanship!"

"Open the bathrooms!" one woman shouted as several women shouted in solidarity with her.

"Okay I can see this isn't going over the way I hoped," the announcer said. "Everybody start the fireworks!"

Suddenly the fireworks began thundering and lighting up the sky as the song Don't Dream It's Over began playing.

"Everybody storm the men's room!" Jill shouted as the woman began getting up and shouting as they all charged towards the bathrooms. "Let the revolution of the bladder proletariat begin!"

"What does that mean?" Britney said as she popped her gum once again.

"Google it," Jill said as she led a crowd of unruly glowing women towards the bathrooms.

Dennis was standing at the door to the men's room and he felt practically blinded by the onslaught of the glowing women, so much so that he was putting his arm up in front of his eyes.

"Well ladies I can't let you in there, that's the men's room!" Dennis shouted.

"It's nothing I haven't seen before," Brenda said as she stood there tapping her foot and giving angry scowls.

"Let us through Dennis, this is a revolution, so we're not asking, we're telling," Jill said. "We will not be tolerating your patriarchal bathroom gestapo tactics any longer! Liberate the ladies room, or the men's room, whatever; we aren't picky when we are this bursting!"

As Dennis stood there looking at the huge crowd of women storming the door he simply stepped aside and pointed to the door. "Ladies first," he said as he got out of the way and all of the women charged into the restroom. "Do so in an orderly manner ladies!" Dennis shouted but he realized that his days as a bathroom line monitor were over and when all of this was over he was going to have a lot of cleaning to do in the bathroom.

As the women commandeered the men's room while the fireworks continue to explode overhead Jill came out triumphantly with her friends with a big smile on her face and all the other women began clapping and cheering.

"Well Jill it looks like you finally got to be a revolutionary," Henry said. "How does it feel?"

Jill patted herself in the bladder area. "You know it feels pretty damn empty."

Everyone burst out laughing as they continued watching the fireworks together.

"Hey look Jill it's a shooting star," James said as he pointed to the sky. "You already got your wish to be a revolutionary, complete with your own fireworks display, but hey I'm sure there's something else you would like to wish for right?"

Jill looked up at the shooting star that was just barely visible through all of the explosions of the fireworks, closed her eyes and wished deeply that she had the same power that all of her friends had, that half of the world now had. When she opened her eyes and still didn't see anyone glowing she simply shrugged her shoulders.

"Well it was worth a try," Jill said as she laughed.

"What did you wish for Jill?" Susan asked.

"If she tells it won't come true," Britney said as she once again popped her gum. "You know what I think I'll go to the bathroom too."

"But I thought you didn't have to go to the bathroom in public ever?" Mark asked.

"Yeah but I want to be part of the revolution, Jill's revolution of the pole dancers," Britney said with a giggle.

"It's proletariat!" Jill said as she threw up her arms in

exasperation and shook her head. "You know what, have your moment, and join the revolution sister!"

"I'm a revolutionary," Britney said as she ran towards the bathroom, tripped on her own feet and fell flat on her face as all of her friends laughed. She simply looked up and laughed as well and began giggling and popping her gum.

"Well Jill I hope that you are happy," Dennis said as they got on the bus ride home. "After your little revolution got televised I am sure that no women will ever tolerate the bathroom monitoring line system again, and you have effectively put me out of work."

"Don't worry in my perfect socialist utopia you will be taken care of, you just might have to wait on line for something for a change," Jill said as she laughed. "But for what it's worth I'm very happy."

Jill looked out the window and she could still see the shooting star and she closed her eyes and wished once again but she could see that no one else was glowing on the bus, but she didn't care, after the day she had had she could be satisfied with being a revolutionary, even if she would never be a psychic. Besides, with people like Britney in the world she didn't even really have to be a psychic to be convincing and she felt she could live with that.

It was a very good night.

Epilogue

Jill woke up the next morning after her exhausting 15 minutes of fame at the festival and she wanted to see if she had gone viral on the Internet yet, but as soon as she woke up she realized something more urgent.

"Wow I really have to pee right now!" Jill said as she ran into the bathroom and looked at the mirror on the wall before doing a double take. As she stared at herself in the mirror that was sitting in front of her right across from the toilet, she noticed that she had a bright red glow around her entire body. "No, it couldn't be," she said as she looked at herself in the mirror to see that she was indeed glowing bright red. But she didn't have time to contemplate that, if she didn't sit on the toilet right away in just a moment her bladder would explode and she would have a big mess to clean up.

Jill jerked down her pajamas and sat on the toilet and

continued staring at herself in the mirror as she began peeing really loudly. As she did so she saw her color going from red, to orange, to green, to blue, to yellow and finally to a pure white color as she finished up.

As she flushed the toilet and wiped herself she then stood there and looked at herself in the mirror, now no longer glowing except for a dim white. She thought that maybe it was just a fluke, maybe she had just imagined it, so she decided to look out the window to the street below and lo and behold she could see women on the street, some of whom were glowing brightly of all different colors of the rainbow.

Jill turned back to the mirror, looked at herself, spun around, snapped her fingers and smiled. "I'm a God damn motherfucking superhero bitches!"

Bonus Stories
Your Bladder and You

Sometime in the 1950s in a typical American town.

"Class today we have a very special video for everyone," Mr. Whitaker said.

"Is it going to be another video about how all we have to do to survive a nuclear Holocaust is duck under our desk and cover our heads?" Johnny said as he raised his hand.

"No Johnny, this is actually going to be an informative video about the changes that your body is going through. Recently there has been something of a change in human evolution and we felt that the best way to address this would be through an informational video in the schools. So today the boys and the girls are going to go to separate classrooms and see separate videos about the strange changes you might be noticing. So all of the girls please get up and go to Miss Emily's class to see your video. The boys can stay here and they will watch their video. Now this might be awkward, so I don't want any giggling or anything like that."

Once all the girls had left the classroom Mr. Whitaker began playing the boys video.

"Hello patriotic Americans," the man in the video said. "You boys might have been noticing some strange changes going on with your bodies lately but you should not be alarmed. Apparently there has been an evolutionary change in mankind so that now every single man has been noticing women in a different way. You might have been noticing that your female classmates are suddenly glowing all the time."

All of the boys in the class started nodding and smiling at one another.

"I just want to reassure all of you that it's perfectly normal for you to see your female classmates glowing all sorts of different colors," the man on the video said. "The reason why women are glowing now all of the sudden is because they have to go to the bathroom."

Several boys in the class began snickering and laughing.

"Hey listen to the video or I will send you to the principal," Mr. Whitaker said. "If anyone else laughs I am going to give them detention."

"Some of you may find these changes to be rather alarming but I assure you that they are perfectly natural," the man in the video said. "Every woman now glows when her bladder gets to a certain level of fullness, with the color changing in color and intensity the greater her need to go to the bathroom is. You may find yourself suddenly more attracted to women suddenly because you find them glowing all the time. There is nothing abnormal about this, but a proper gentleman would not mention these things to a lady. Ladies are very modest and don't like people commenting on the fullness of their bladder based on how they are glowing. So if you see a female classmate who is glowing brightly be kind to her because she needs to go to the bathroom very badly. But also be polite and do not bring up this fact if she does not bring it up first. Simply help her find a bathroom while trying not to make obvious reference to the fact that you know her bladder is extremely full.

"Now there are some of you might find yourself unnaturally interested in this glowing phenomenon that you notice around your female classmates. There is nothing in and of itself abnormal about that, but you do have to realize that the reason women are glowing is because they have to go to the bathroom. You don't want to be attracted to someone simply because of the fullness of their bladder do you?

"Some of you may even take these unnatural urges to dangerous extremes however, and that would make you to be abnormal. It is not fully normal to be attracted to a woman based on the size or fullness of her bladder. It is also abnormal if you try to cause your female classmates to wet themselves. That is why you should always show proper decorum to your female classmates and never attempt to get them to wet their pants. You wouldn't want them to make you wet your pants, would you?

"Some of you may even feel increasingly strong abnormal urges the more you see your female classmates glowing. This new change presents a challenge to all of us in polite society. There are some people who might even be tempted to touch themselves based on the excitement that comes with seeing a female classmate glowing because of a full bladder.

"Don't touch yourselves! As you all know masturbation is a form of mental illness and that if you do it excessively you could grow hair on your palms and you might even go blind. People who touch themselves excessively always end up going insane and becoming social menaces. You don't want to be a menace to your fellow classmates do you?

"Of course you don't! That is why I encourage every patriotic and normal American boy not to give into the urge to touch themselves just because they see their female classmates glowing brightly and beautifully. It is okay to comment that a woman has a healthy glow and that she looks pretty, but remember why she is glowing and try not to think about it too much, because that way lays madness!"

Mr. Whitaker turned off the tape. "I hope you all found that informative and educational. Does anybody have any questions?"

Johnny wanted to raise his hands as this video gave him a whole lot of questions.

"Is the fact that women are glowing because of radioactive fallout from nuclear tests?" Wayne asked.

"Nobody knows why women are glowing all of the sudden when their bladders are full," Mr. Whitaker said. "It's a strange and unexplained new phenomenon but I am sure that there is a rational explanation behind it."

"Like what?" Wayne asked as he kept his hand up.

"Well there's a whole bunch of scientific theories on why this might be, but I think that the most rational explanation is it's because of a communist plot," Mr. Whitaker said. "People always said that fluoride in the water was good for us but I think that now we are seeing that there might be an ulterior motive behind putting fluoride in the water."

"But Mr. Whitaker why would the Communists want to put fluoride in the water to make women glow when their bladders are full?"

"How the hell should I know, they are communists, they're crazy! Maybe they want to make our women glow in the dark so that they can easily see them in the nighttime when they invade. If the women are all glowing it will be easier for the Communists to make off with them to send them to all of their crazy breeding camps, and they figure that if all the boys are distracted watching all the girls glowing all the time it will allow them to get the drop on us. Does anyone else have any other questions?"

Johnny and Wayne looked at each other and they shook their heads.

"Good now let us get back to our lesson," Mr. Whitaker said as he wrote on the blackboard civil rights, is it trouble ahead?

"I wonder if the girls' video is equally as confusing and strange," Johnny whispered to Wayne.

"Now girls we're going to show you an informative video called your bladder and you," Miss Emily said. "Please hold all questions until the end. I hope that you find this video as informative as our last sex specific video how to find a rich husband and make him happy when he gets home from work."

Miss Emily began playing the video.

"Hi ladies," the woman on the video said. "I'm here to address a strange new phenomenon that you might have noticed. You might have been noticing that your male classmates and teachers and other male associates might have been acting strangely lately. This is because of the strange new phenomenon whereby it seems that women are now glowing but that the glowing is only obvious to men. You are probably wondering why the men are acting so strange as you cannot see what they see.

"Nobody knows why this new phenomenon has occurred, but what we do know is that many men are now being very distracted by the fact that you ladies are glowing, and naturally some of you are probably feeling self-conscious about this, as well you should!

"Now of course ladies all of us want to be modest and not be distracting to the men while they do all sorts of important jobs, but unfortunately we have no control over the fact that when our bladders get full we begin glowing. This might attract unwanted male attention and you are probably wondering how you should respond to a man who might be acting strangely because of the fact that your bladder is full and that you are glowing brightly. What exactly is the polite thing to do if you find yourself in a situation where your bladder is full and you are glowing?

"Firstly it's important to stay hydrated, so you don't want to dehydrate yourself just because you give off a glow when your bladders are full, as that would not be healthy. But at the same time as a good woman you do not want to be driving the men crazy with your incessant glowing. A proper lady doesn't want men to know when she has to go to the bathroom, but unfortunately that is no longer possible.

"So what you should do ladies if you find yourself with a full bladder is to try to relieve yourself without drawing any attention to yourself. A woman with a full bladder can be very distracting to her male companions and for that reason you should try to take care of a full bladder without drawing more attention to yourself.

"Of course if you are not in a position to relieve your full bladder the proper thing to do is to try to ignore the situation and not draw attention to the fact that your bladder is full. Obviously the men in your life will know that your bladder is full, but the proper thing to do is to try not to address it because it's awkward and uncomfortable for everyone.

"Another thing is that many of the men in your life might be suddenly giving you a lot of unwanted attention because of your full bladders. There are some men who might find the idea of a woman who suddenly glows, particularly at night time, extremely attractive. But you should know that these men are extremely abnormal and you should try your best to ignore them because they might have sick urges and impure thoughts because of your full bladder. You should try to avoid provoking these men at all costs because it's up to the women to make sure that the men control themselves.

"So in conclusion ladies if you find yourself with a full bladder that you cannot relieve don't incite the men to craziness by mentioning it, simply hold it in and try to regard the world with a smile, everyone loves it when a woman smiles. The modest thing to do is to hold a full bladder until you can relieve it and to try not to be a nuisance by letting your bladder be a distraction to others. So remember ladies, if you can't relieve it, hold it and say nothing, because that is the proper thing to do."

"Do you have any questions?" Miss Emily said as she turned off the video.

Elizabeth wanted to ask a question but she felt too awkward asking a question about such an improper topic, as did most of the rest of the girls in the class who simply looked at each other nervously and uncomfortably.

"Good now let us get back to our lesson," Miss Emily said as she wrote on the board feminism, is it a communist plot like everything else?

Later that day at recess Johnny and Wayne couldn't help but notice that a lot of the girls were glowing.

"Do you see the way that Elizabeth glows, she's really pretty," Johnny said.

"You're not having abnormal feelings towards her because she's glowing are you?" Wayne said.

"No, of course not! I'm a normal patriotic American just like everybody else. I'm not one of those guys who go after women who are glowing all the time."

"Okay that's good, because you wouldn't want to be with a woman who was glowing all the time because that will make her an easy target when the communists invade."

"You don't really think that this is a communist plot do you?"

"Who knows, those Russians are crazy like Mr. Whitaker said. They probably want to turn us all into perverts who will be easily distracted by glowing women with full bladders. But we are totally normal boys who are not going to be turned on by a little bit of glowing from women."

"Hi Johnny," Elizabeth said as she came over with a bright glow around her that made her look like she had a halo, like she was actually an angel or something.

"Elizabeth, hi!" Johnny said feeling nervous and trying not to get an erection by thinking of his mother, the American flag and apple pie in order to stay calm.

"I was just wondering Johnny, if you're not doing anything this weekend, do you think you would like to go see a monster movie with me?"

"Sure Elizabeth, I would love to go to the movies with you. I can pick you up at around 7 PM."

"That sounds great; I'll be looking forward to it."

As Elizabeth walked off Johnny and Wayne looked at each other.

"I can't believe Elizabeth agreed to go on a date with me!" Johnny shouted.

"Are you really sure that you want to go out with Elizabeth?" Wayne asked.

"I am as sure of that as I am sure that America will have a city on the moon by 1965."

"I'm just saying that I can't help but notice that she seemed to be flaunting the fact that she was glowing. It's almost like she abstained from going to the bathroom specifically to make herself more attractive."

"It's not like that at all! You know I'm not a weird guy like that, I'm no communist, I'm a Yankee first and foremost. You know I check my closet every night for communist spies and hidden microphones like every normal American boy."

Wayne shook his head. "I don't know, many a good man has been corrupted by a woman and now women are glowing, they are practically radioactive."

"Well I'm not going to give up my date with Elizabeth; I have been looking forward to this for my entire life. I can't believe she actually asked if I wanted to go on a date with her."

"Just you be careful, you never know what a glowing woman could be up to. And if I were you I would go easy on the tap water."

That night all Johnny could think about was Elizabeth glowing brightly like a vision straight from heaven. When he woke up he found that he had had one of those embarrassing dreams again, one so intense he almost thought that he had wet the bed.

"I'm not an abnormal freak," Johnny said as he woke up from his dream to realize that he had a very wet dream. But he was trying to convince himself of that because he wasn't quite sure. He didn't think that there was anything abnormal about his attraction towards

Elizabeth. He had been attracted to her since before women started glowing all of the sudden, although he had to admit that he was suddenly more attracted to her than ever before.

When he got up he cleaned up his bed and put on his best outfit and wanted to get to Elizabeth's house as early as possible. When she answered the door he couldn't help but notice that she was dressed in a bright pink dress and she had a faint greenish glow around her, which he knew meant that she already had to go to the bathroom.

"Elizabeth, hi, how are you," Johnny said, once again trying to control his excitement at seeing her bright and glowing.

"I'm doing great Johnny, how about you?" Elizabeth said with a smile.

"I'm doing wonderful," Johnny said unable to help the fact that he was getting extremely excited by the fact that she was already glowing. "Are you ready to go or is there anything that you want to get or do before we leave?" He was trying to subtly indicate that maybe she wanted to use the bathroom because her glowing was driving him completely wild.

"No Johnny I think that everything's fine, I think we should get to the movies right away," she said as they began walking to the movies.

"Two for the double feature," Johnny said as he purchased the tickets. It was a double billing of The Communists from Outer Space and Communist Invaders from Mars.

"Let's get something at the concession stand," Elizabeth said as Johnny got them both large popcorns and very large sodas with a free refill option.

As they sat down to start watching the movie Johnny couldn't help but notice that Elizabeth was glowing more brightly and was starting to turn orange, which he knew meant that she had to go to the bathroom desperately bad, and yet she seemed to be fully calm and composed.

Johnny was barely paying attention to the movie because he couldn't help but notice that Elizabeth was glowing so brightly and all he could think about was how she had not been to the bathroom this entire time.

By the time the first movie was over Elizabeth was now glowing bright orange and Johnny couldn't help but notice that large numbers of people were staring at her, or at least the men were anyway.

"I'm going to go use the bathroom," Johnny said as he got up during the intermission. "Is there anything else you want at the concession stand?"

"Yeah, can you get a refill on this for me," Elizabeth said as she handed him her empty soda cup.

"Sure," Johnny said as he took her empty cup, used the bathroom and got her cup refilled.

"Hey Johnny, how is your date going?" Wayne asked.

"Wayne, what are you doing here?" Johnny asked.

"I just came to see a movie like everybody else, but I couldn't help but notice that your girlfriend was distracting a lot of people in the theater with her glowing," Wayne said as he shook his head.

"There's nothing wrong with a woman who glows."

"I don't know it's kind of immodest, do you think that she might be a communist or a feminist or a communist feminist, possibly from the planet Venus?"

"Dammit Wayne for the last time, Elizabeth isn't a communist, she isn't a feminist and she isn't an alien invader or all three."

"Are you sure, those things usually come in threes, haven't you been paying attention to the movie?"

"I just want to get back to my date; Elizabeth is waiting for me to give her a refill of her soda."

Wayne shook his head as Johnny ran back to the theater. "She's going to be the death of him, that glowing bladder hussy!"

As Johnny sat back down next to Elizabeth and gave her back her once again full soda he couldn't help but notice that she started rapidly drinking it. Much like with the first movie he found himself barely able to concentrate on the highly cerebral plot about a bunch of alien communist body snatchers from Mars replacing people at the highest levels of government.

"The nerve of that woman," a man said as they looked at Elizabeth who was now glowing bright red. "Her glowing is distracting me from the movie."

Johnny couldn't help but notice that everyone in the theater seemed to be staring at he and Elizabeth but Elizabeth seemed like she was just sitting there calmly watching the movie, even though he knew her bladder must be ready to explode. The fact that she could sit there so calmly while her bladder was that full was driving Johnny absolutely wild and making him think that maybe alien communists had been doing something to his brain waves after all.

Finally the movie was over and he noticed that Elizabeth had long since finished her large soda.

"I think I'm going to go use the little boys room," Johnny said. Johnny went into the bathroom and splashed himself with some cold water to try and get himself under control. The fact that Elizabeth was now glowing as bright as the sun was really making him wild. The thought that her bladder was so full was getting him really hot and bothered.

"How did the date go," Wayne said coming up behind Johnny and scaring him.

"Wayne you startled me, I thought you were an alien communist from Mars!" Johnny shouted.

Wayne laughed. "Well I'm no alien communist from Mars, but I'm thinking that maybe your girlfriend is. What type of human being has a bladder capacity that extreme?"

"There is nothing abnormal about Elizabeth," Johnny said. "She's a lovely modest young girl and she probably just doesn't want to say anything about the fact that she has to go to the bathroom. She's probably just shy about it; lots of girls are shy about it."

"I don't know, she still seems kind of suspicious to me."

"Well she's waiting for me, so I don't want to keep her waiting."

When Johnny came out of the restroom he could see that Elizabeth was standing there still glowing bright red.

"Do you need to use the bathroom before we leave?" Johnny asked not wanting to sound rude but at the same time astonished that she still hadn't used the bathroom.

"Oh it's out of order," Elizabeth said as she stood there and Johnny could see that she was very slightly crossing her legs at the ankles. "But that's okay; we will be home in a little while."

"I thought that maybe we could go look at the town from up on the mountain side," Johnny said not wanting to explicitly mention that he wanted to take her to make out point.

"You know that sounds rather nice Johnny, I would love to," Elizabeth said as the two of them began walking. As they walked

Johnny noticed that everyone was staring directly at Elizabeth because she had been lighting up the night like a supernova. Going around with a woman on his arm that everyone was looking at made Johnny feel like he was special and important, and he couldn't help but grow more excited every second that he kept Elizabeth away from the bathroom.

Finally they got to the point where they could see the entire city and they saw lots of other people were making out, but a lot of them were looking at Johnny and Elizabeth, probably because of the fact that Elizabeth was lighting up the night.

Eventually Johnny leaned forward and began kissing Elizabeth. She was so bright that he was finding he was seeing spots, but he didn't even care. He could feel Elizabeth shaking and trembling as he kissed her and he knew that she must be getting close to the point where she needed to use the bathroom and the fact that she had put it off all night long was driving him completely out of his mind.

After making out for a while they knew that they had to get home but Johnny went as slow as possible seeing how long he could keep Elizabeth away from the bathroom. As they walked down the street several men put their arms up to their eyes and several women looked at the men with jealous stares as they all stared at Elizabeth.

"I guess I will see you in school on Monday," Johnny said as Elizabeth kissed him and smiled.

"Thank you for a lovely evening," Elizabeth said as she smiled and closed the door and immediately ran towards the bathroom, quickly sat down on the toilet and finally relieved herself as she moaned a sigh of relief as she looked in the mirror. "Modest my ass, it's time to shine! My glow brings all the boys to the yard."

Johnny practically ran home and ran past his parents, ran into his bedroom, locked the door and began furiously masturbating to thoughts of Elizabeth and her bursting bladder and it didn't take long before he had made a mess of things.

As he lay back in bed looking up at the ceiling and feeling extremely relaxed he simply shook his head. "I don't care if I do go blind and grow hair on my palms, I'm proud to be abnormal!"

Wayne was looking in through the window and shaking his head. "It looks like we've lost another one to the communist invasion," Wayne said as he walked down the street.

"Hi Wayne," said Cindy, a girl he had always had a crush on and who at the moment was glowing bright red and twirling her fingers through her hair. "What are you doing out late at night? I was wondering if maybe you wanted to do something?"

As Wayne stood there looking at the love of his life glowing like a firecracker in the sky he couldn't help but think that she might be an alien or a communist or a feminist or maybe even all three, but at that moment he didn't care.

"Cindy I would love to," Wayne said as he smiled and offered Cindy a drink.

<u>Desperation Aura Interrogation</u>

Karen was at the protest march protesting police brutality but it was a really hot day and she found herself drinking bottle after bottle of water. It didn't take long for all of that water to find its way to her bladder, which was starting to grow uncomfortably fuller by the moment.

"Hey I can see you are glowing, you must have to pee pretty bad!" her friend Russell said.

"You know that I am self-conscious about the fact that you can tell how badly I have to pee just by reading my aura!" Karen said as she crossed her legs.

Russell shook his head and laughed. "Hey I can't help it, you know that every guy can now see an aura around every woman when she has to go to the bathroom, and right now you are glowing bright green so you must be getting rather uncomfortable."

"Kind of, do you know where you there is a bathroom around here?" Karen asked.

Russell shook his head. "I just went and peed in the bushes when nobody was looking."

"It's times like these I do wish that I had a penis," Karen said as she crossed her legs more tightly. "I really really need a bathroom!"

"Well why don't you just go pee in the bushes and have a squat?"

"Well for one thing I'm not going to pee where everybody can see what I am doing, because I am self-conscious just knowing people know that I have to go to the bathroom, let along seeing me do it. And secondly there are lots of cops around who might arrest me. It figures that at a protest rally for protesting police brutality there are a lot of police here who are probably willing to get rather brutal."

Russell shook his head. "I'm sure they would probably just enjoy the show. I mean what cop hasn't had a bathroom emergency where they just had to pee on the side of the road?"

"But I'm guessing that the lady tops don't get to go as much as the guys do," Karen said as she hopped up and down in place. "Doesn't any place here have an open bathroom?"

Russell shook his head once again. "No, you know that they closed all of the places and the places that do have open bathrooms want you to buy something first, and then there is usually a long line and the toilets are less than appealing."

"Why did I drink so much water?!" Karen said as she shuffled her feet from side to side. "I think that I'm going to have to get to a bathroom soon or else I'm just going to have to go home."

"You're not going to leave now are you; the protest is just kicking into high gear. Don't you want to make a stand against police brutality?"

"Right now I just want to take a stand against the brutal pressure in my bladder!" Karen crossed her legs tightly and bent at the knees as she looked around and began shaking. "I have to go so bad."

"Yeah you're definitely in the orange; you are full-blown desperate right now!" Russell took a sip of his bottle of water. "Would you like something to drink?"

"Very funny smart guy!" Karen said as she gritted her teeth. She had to pee and she knew that she wasn't going to be able to wait that much longer.

"I could finish up this bottle and then maybe you could pee in the bottle and you could hurl it at the police if they get too rough."

"This is a peaceful protest; I'm pretty sure if I hurl a bottle of urine at the police they are probably not going to react very kindly."

Russell shrugged his shoulders. "Oh well, it's your bladder, I guess you'll just have to hold it, but I can tell you that every guy now can see you glowing bright and shining and I think that a lot of people are staring at you."

"Don't tell me that, you know how self-conscious I am about that!"

"But I can't help it, it's very obvious that you are glowing like you're about to explode."

"I am about to explode dammit!" Karen said practically going out of her mind. It was bad enough that she had to go to the bathroom, but she knew that every guy in the vicinity knew that she had to go to the bathroom, many of whom were peeing off in the bushes and were probably enjoying every minute of her urinary discomfort.

Russell laughed. "I have to admit this is actually rather entertaining, even more entertaining than the protest rally. I can see that a lot of other women are glowing as well. That's what you should have all done, you should have made a stand against police brutality by all drinking a lot before coming to the rally and then blinding them with your desperate auras!"

"Somehow I feel that if we did that that would end up being the focus of all the attention. It wouldn't be shedding light on police brutality."

"Yes it would, you would be blinding them, blinding them with the light of truth or justice, the light that just happens to be emanating from your enormously full bladders!"

"No, it's just like ever since this happened all of the focus is on the fact that women are now glowing when they have to pee really bad. People can't take anything we do seriously because it's all about; look at that woman she's glowing. It's now no longer jokes about being that time of the month, it's hey look at that woman she's glowing like her bladder's about to explode, or no wonder she's grouchy, look how badly she has to pee! PMS now stands for piss myself soon! So if we all came to the protest march glowing and blinding the police with our full bladders it would just be lots of jokes about all of these women getting ready to piss themselves."

"Actually I could see that as a headline, women pissed off about police brutality come to piss off!"

"I can see the budding journalist in you already. But right now I just really need to find a bathroom as soon as possible or I'm going to go completely out of my mind!"

Karen was about to try to sneak off to find a bathroom when all of the sudden someone hurled a bottle of what looked like a yellow liquid that hit a police officer right in the face.

"Take that you pigs!" somebody shouted.

"I bet it was you who threw that," the police officer said as they came over by Karen. "It was you, wasn't it! You just hurled a bottle of piss in my face!"

Karen shook her head. "Look officer you can see that I am clearly glowing, so obviously I haven't pissed very recently."

"But I never said it was your piss that was in the bottle, you could have been throwing somebody else's piss, like his piss," the police officer said as he pointed to Russell.

"Hey I have nothing against police officers," Russell said putting his hands up defensively. "I'm just at this rally because I am a budding journalist and I want to document the whole thing. For the record I have never thrown piss in anyone's face, whether they are in a position of authority or not."

The police officer shook his head. "Well it came from right over here and right from where you are standing, I'm afraid I'm going to have to take you in for questioning," the police officer said as he handcuffed Karen.

"But I didn't do anything; this is a violation of my rights!" Karen said as the police officer dragged her away and took her to a small room and sat her down in a small chair and handcuffed her to the chair. "At least let me use the bathroom!"

"If you wanted to use the bathroom you shouldn't have thrown piss in my face!" the police officer said as he shook his head.

"But I didn't throw piss in your face, that's what I am telling you!" Karen said as she squirmed around in her seat crossing and uncrossing her legs a hundred miles a minute as she tapped her feet loudly on the floor.

"Hey red alert," another police officer said as he came into the room with a smile.

"Hey Officer Dan," the first police officer said as he slapped him high-five.

"What's up Officer Frank," Dan said with a smile.

"This so-called peaceful protester hit me in the face with a bottle of piss."

"But I'm telling you it wasn't me!" Karen shouted. "You can tell by looking at me that I am glowing bright red and that I am going out of my mind with a full bladder, obviously I haven't peed anytime recently."

Officer Dan shook his head. "Like I said it wasn't necessarily your piss that you threw at me. Besides with how fast you seem to need to go to the bathroom you could have been standing there drinking all day, filling bottle after bottle of piss so that you can barrage the police, make the boys in blue the boys in yellow. You think you can intimidate us by throwing urine in our faces?"

"What is this, an interrogation?" Karen said as she squirmed in her seat struggling to get comfortable but not being able to take the enormous pressure off of her bladder.

"That's exactly what it is!" Dan shouted.

"Well can you at least let me go to the bathroom first," Karen said crossing her legs tightly. "I'm absolutely dying in here!"

Dan and Frank looked at each other and shook their heads before then looked back at her. "Like I said you should have thought of that before you threw piss at me. But we will let you go to the bathroom, once you admit what has gone on and tell us the full truth."

"But I'm already telling you the truth!" Karen shouted. "I'm telling you that wasn't my urine!"

"Good, so you admit that it was someone else's urine that you threw at me then," officer Dan said with a smile.

"No, that's not what I said; you're putting words in my mouth!" Karen shouted.

Officer Dan and Officer Frank shook their heads and looked back at her.

"Well that's not all that we're going to put in your mouth then," Frank said as he took a large bottle of water, unscrewed the cap and put it up to Karen's mouth. "Drink it, all of it!"

"What?" Karen said as she tried to squirm away from it. "But my bladder is already completely full!"

"You heard the officer, drink up," Dan said. "If you think it's so funny to use your urine maliciously we are going to teach you what it's like to have to control what you do with your urine. Now start drinking!"

Karen was so frightened right now she felt like she could practically piss herself, and she knew the drinking more was certainly going to not help that situation, but seeing as she was at a protest for police brutality she knew that some cops certainly weren't above using unlawful methods of getting her to talk, and she didn't know what they were going to do if she didn't cooperate, so she immediately started drinking the bottle of water until she had drank every last drop.

"There, I drank it, now can I go to the bathroom?" Karen said.

Dan and Frank laughed as they sat down across from her.

"I think that we should just sit here and wait until she confesses," Frank said as he smiled and looked at Dan who smiled and nodded back. "Besides she has a nice healthy glow to her, we could practically read by it!"

That was when Karen realized a terrible truth. "You sick bastards, you're just taking advantage of me to satisfy your sick glow fetish! This is police brutality, now you can see why I was so motivated to protest! Well that and I think the police brutally murdering people for minor violations based on the color of their skin is wrong, but now this on top of that!"

Dan and Frank shook their heads. "We can wait," Dan said. "The question is how long can you wait?"

Karen put her head down and shook her head. "You know this is exactly why people are protesting, I don't mean specifically about the urine suppression right now, I just mean it's bad cops like you give the good cops a bad name and this is why people don't respect the police more. If you would do something as simple as let me go to the bathroom I wouldn't complain that you are violating my rights. I have a right to use the bathroom. I should be free to pee!"

"Like I said, we can wait," Dan said.

"But I have to pee and I have to pee right now!" Karen said as she bit down on her lip and squirmed in her seat. "Please just let me go to the bathroom and I won't say anything about this, I swear!"

Frank and Dan looked at each other and smiled.

"Maybe she would relax more if we played some soothing music," Frank said as he went over to a laptop. "How about sounds of the ocean, rushing waterfalls?"

Immediately the room filled with the loud sound of crashing waterfalls cascading all over the place.

"I'm not going to give in and confess to something that I didn't do just because you are torturing me," Karen said trying to drown out the sound of the waterfalls, but finding that her legs were shaking like crazy and she could barely sit still.

"Well I know you can't see it the way we can see it on you, but I have to pee as well," Frank said as he went to the corner and began peeing loudly into a metal bucket.

Now Karen was sweating bullets and shaking in her seat and she knew she couldn't last much longer.

"Wow she's blinding me now, I don't think she's going to last much longer," Dan said as he covered up his eyes and put down his dark sunglasses.

Just as Karen thought that she was about to wet herself that was when another officer, a tall African-American woman, came into the room.

"What the hell are you boys doing in here?!" she said shaking her head. "Don't tell me you're doing this again, you are forcing a woman to have a full bladder and then interrogating her and torturing her just so that you can get your kicks from letting her glow. Release her right now I'm going to report you again!"

"Damn Shawna you always ruin our fun," Dan said as he took the handcuffs off and let Karen get up.

"Where's the bathroom?!" Karen shouted as she grabbed herself tightly crossing her legs furiously and hopping in place.

Shawna pointed her down the hall and Karen practically knocked people over on the way down, except she didn't want to end up finding herself arrested again for assaulting a police officer, so she walked slowly, got to the bathroom, slammed the door, ripped her pants down and sat her ass on the toilet and peed for what seemed like an eternity as she screamed at the top of her lungs.

When she came out of the bathroom everyone in the police department was looking at her, and several of the men looked like they had lecherous smiles on her face, one covering his crotch area with a folder.

"Get a hobby!" Karen shouted knowing that she was now no longer glowing. She went over to Shawna and smiled. "Thank you, it's good to know that there are still good cops out there looking out for people's rights."

Shawna nodded and smiled. "Truth be told is I have sympathy for you protesters because you want to make us more accountable and hold jerks like Frank and Dan accountable to their actions. The fact is that you're not the first person they have done it to and likely not the last, and there are a whole bunch of police officers in the department that have been taking advantage of the fact that they know women have to pee to torture them like this. It's an unspoken thing and I have been trying to expose it for a while now. They've even taken advantage of the fact that I had to pee while on duty. You have no idea how annoying it is to work with a bunch of guys who know that you are ready to explode all day, but because you have to do your duty you can't find a way to a bathroom break. You try holding a full bladder all day while patrolling the streets while the guys just go pee on the side of the road even though that they know public urination is a crime."

"I guess it's a matter of who will Peeolice the police," Karen said as she laughed. "Get it?"

Shawna rolled her eyes. "Yes I get it. But I really wish that I could expose this sick underground of police officers taking advantage of women because they have this sick fetish for seeing them glow when their bladders are about to explode."

"Actually I kind of know a budding journalist and this could be the type of story that would really help his career, and I think he would blow the lid off of this, no pun intended," Karen said as she laughed. "Get it, lid, because of toilet seats and, oh forget it."

A short while later.

"Well I did blow the lid off of it," Russell said as he handed Karen the article that he wrote exposing police brutality against women's bladders.

"Women are incredibly pissed," Karen said. "In fact they are glowing with rage over this latest outrage –"

Karen put the paper down.

"What, it's clever wordplay," Russell said shaking his head. "It is a serious article though, and I just hope that it is given the seriousness that it deserves."

"I have to admit though I'm a little bit self-conscious over the fact that you told everybody about how I had to go to the bathroom all day and what happened to me," Karen said. "I mean I get that you had to tell the story as is, but I'm still embarrassed."

"But shouldn't be, you're the head of the #PeeToo movement," Russell said with a laugh.

"Oh you're not serious, that's what you are actually calling this?" Karen said as she read the article shaking her head. "No one's ever going to take this seriously!"

"Hey I thought it was a clever hashtag that would get people to come out in support of you. Lots of women have had their bladders tortured by police officers and now maybe they will come forward thanks to you."

Karen shook her head. "Well I doubt that this is going to lead to any real life substantial change in the world, in fact am almost hoping that maybe people will forget about this now."

"But don't you want justice for what happened to you?"

"Of course I do, but I don't exactly want to be head of something called the #PeeToo movement!"

"Silence only enables the oppressor, you can't be neutral on these matters, staying silent is never a good idea."

"I can't believe that you actually just quoted a Holocaust survivor Elie Wiesel in regards to something about the bathroom, and yet at the same time you kind of make a good point. And that's just making me even angrier about this! Whatever though, I am sure that in a week or two this will blow over anyway."

A week or two later…

"I can't believe that I am at the head of something called the million bladder March," Karen said as she stood there glowing and holding herself and looking at all of the other women around her doing likewise.

"Well hey, with all these many women glowing there's not a man in America who is going to be able to not be blinded by the light of truth now," Russell said as he put on his sunglasses.

Karen shook her head. "Well maybe you are right, maybe people actually will take this seriously, even though it's involving urine. There is just really one thing that I really really wish you had considered when you plan this whole crazy March."

"What's that?"

"Why couldn't you have planned for bathroom availability?!" Karen said as she looked over the crowd of glowing women, seeing not a single bathroom available in sight.

Russell laughed. "Well I guess that's a wash, get it a wash because everybody's going to pee and flood this place."

"Shut up!" Karen said as she reached for the empty sports

bottle at her side and started thinking of a place where she could go to fill it discreetly, not to throw at a police officer, but just because she really needed it.

Some Words from the Author

I am extremely pleased with this novel as this was my first full-length female desperation themed novel that I have written. It is longer than both of my previous two novellas combined (The Great Locked Ladies Room Caper and The Terrible, Horrible, No Good, Very Desperate Bus Ride). I originally didn't think that it would be as long as it was and that it would probably just be a short one like my other two novellas, but then this is the first desperation themed book that I wrote involving speculative fiction themes, which as a novelist of science fiction, fantasy and horror is the genre I am most natural at writing. However it was inevitable that eventually I would combine my fetish with my speculative themes and this is the first instance where I have done so and I am quite pleased with the outcome.

I don't remember when I first had this idea but I had it for a very long time before I decided to turn it into an actual novel, probably at least a decade or more from my earliest days on various pee fetish boards and chat rooms. For many years I went into pee desperation fetish chats and would tell people about this idea that I had about the idea that people could somehow sense how desperate people were to go to the bathroom in a psychic manner, specifically the ability to read some type of pee aura around a person, which would glow with increasing intensity and brightness the more they had to go to the bathroom, so that there was no way to conceal it from anyone around you, and it would be obvious to everyone, potentially a very embarrassing type of situation. I decided that I would use a color-coded system as far as the glowing went, going from really light colors for when a person was relatively empty with the colors glowing darker colors and with greater intensity the more the person had to go to the bathroom.

When I originally conceived of the idea I thought of sort of a lightbulb appearing over the person's head, but eventually came around to the idea that it would make more sense if the women were glowing over their entire bodies, very specifically an aura. The lightbulb idea seems a little bit silly by comparison. Auras are at least a real concept, whether or not people believe in them.

While I was talking about this idea with many people over the years some pointed out that the desperation would probably be somewhat subjective. Several people brought up the fact that if you saw a woman glowing desperate how did you know how long it would be before she got to the point where she couldn't hold it any longer, seeing as certain people would get desperate at a quicker rate and everyone had different bladder sizes and could hold for different lengths of time. For one person they could hold a very full bladder for a very long time, whereas for another person they might go rapidly through all the colors.

Ultimately I decided that bladder strength would have to be sort of a subjective thing but I figured that the glowing would indicate how full the bladder was specifically. It wouldn't tell you exactly how long the person would be able to hold it for, but it would let you know how badly they needed to go. I had already started writing the novel when I had discussions about this and I decided to incorporate this debate specifically in the chapter where Jill gets in the holding contest with Britney. It was naturally assumed that because her bladder was already much fuller when she started the contest that she would automatically lose, only for them to realize, much to Jill's frustration and embarrassment, that just seeing how full a person's bladder was didn't indicate how long they would be able to hold it. While Jill went rapidly through all of the colors Britney, who had the larger bladder, was able to hold a very full bladder for a much longer time and didn't get desperate as rapidly, teaching Jill and the guys an important lesson in humility so they would not make that mistake a second time.

I eventually decided on the idea that only guys would have the ability because I thought that would create a great deal of conflict and frustration for the main character, who once again is largely based on me and is named after me, like in my previous desperation novellas. Over the course of talking about this I was discussing the idea with several guys who liked the idea of being able to know when women had to go to the bathroom, because it's not always obvious, and that it would be really a cool ability to have. So I thought the fact that Jill's friends, both guys who are into female desperation, would suddenly end up gaining the ability which would make things extremely awkward for her, as well as frustrate her with jealousy over the fact that she herself did not have the ability. So that ultimately became the central conflict of much of the novel.

I also liked the fact that this allowed me to do some satirizing of psychic powers and everything. As a speculative fiction novelist I have always been extremely fascinated by psychic powers and abilities, and I am definitely a believer that psychic power is a real thing, and I have had numerous psychic experiences of my own over the years. However while I believe that there are many legitimate psychics out there, I believe that most commercial psychics are completely and utterly full of it and easily exploit gullible people. So then I thought of how insane it would be if somebody suddenly gained the psychic ability that was so specific to read the person's auras, but instead of telling them their health or their spiritual status or something like that, all that it told them was how badly women had to go to the bathroom. I thought that even real life psychics, or alleged psychics, would probably laugh at the notion of a specific psychic power that was so oddly specific and caters to a specific fetish like knowing how badly women have to go to the bathroom.

Originally when I conceived of the idea I was going to have the sudden psychic abilities be the result of her friends just happening to eat some tainted tacos that somehow end up giving them this weird and unexplained power. So originally I was just going to have her two friends gain the ability and for them to have all sorts of fun with it. But then as I was writing it I started thinking of the implications of what if all men had the ability and the wider implications that would have on society at large.

Once again you can take a simple and somewhat absurd idea that would change the world but when you really start thinking about you think of all the many ways that even something really trivial and strange like this could change society on a large scale.

So I figured that if men suddenly gained this new ability naturally they would take advantage of it and use it mostly against women. The idea that full bladders would cause a person to glow, women specifically, would just be another thing that women had to be self-conscious about. As I said in the chapter: "Women already had enough things to be self-conscious about. We had to worry about our weight, our clothing, our appearance, the way we come across, the way we talk and all these other sexist things that we have to deal with, and now we have to deal with the fact that when we have to go to the bathroom every single man in the vicinity is going to know it. In all honesty I am getting quite sick of it every day."

So I was able to get in some effective commentary on how men take advantage of women and all the sexist implications of men having a special new ability that women did not have, including male politicians taking advantage of female politicians in a debate, men catcalling women based on their bladder size and fullness, little boys teasing little girls about having to go to the bathroom, men trying to get women to wet themselves and eventually men trying to police and control women based on the new ability (bathroom line monitors etc.). And also the fact that many people would blame women for their glowing being a distraction in the way that men now blame women for distracting them by wearing revealing clothing, putting the burden on women rather than just telling men to freaking control themselves.

I also thought about the widespread sexual implications of the idea that suddenly men can see women glowing all the time. I figured that a lot of men who might not be into female pee desperation specifically might be turned on by the idea of women who glow, so I developed this whole concept of a glow fetish that eventually led to glow clubs such as the one that Britney worked at. And eventually it gets to the point where men try to get women stuck in these bladder desperation situations simply because they like the fun of making women glow in the dark.

At the same time however I thought that it served largely as a metaphor for the fact that many people have a fetish for female pee desperation without necessarily even acknowledging it. So having a "glow fetish" is just people's way of openly expressing the fact that they are interested in the idea that women have to go to the bathroom. And even beyond that I think that even people who didn't have a fetish would find the whole thing curious, not just because it would have sexual implications, but also because people I think would be really immature about something like this in general!

I figured I would never address the exact reason why all of this occurred as leaving it unexplained lets people speculate more and go crazy with the idea. I had the evolutionary biologist, the college professor; try to explain things in evolutionary terms, but having no real logical explanation. The idea that it was caused by tacos is put to rest when it starts affecting the entire male population. The supernatural explanation could be a possibility but even the psychic didn't really have any idea why it was happening, even though she correctly predicted that something big was going to happen with all of this. I guess the story sort of inclines towards the idea that it was a supernatural occurrence, but at the same time leave it pretty much open-ended as to what caused it, as I feel that's irrelevant to the greater story about its effects on society at large and on the characters in particular.

I did suggest that there was something perhaps genetic about it by the inclusion of the transgender woman character. Although she had transitioned to female she still had male chromosomes, so that made her both able to have the psychic ability to read other women and their desperation levels while being able to conceal her own. Originally I was going to introduce her earlier and have the fact that there was another woman with this ability but who could not be psychically read herself frustrate Jill more and have her be a female desperation fan who took advantage of Jill while she was in line for the bathroom, but then I didn't get around to introducing her until later. But she provides some type of plausible explanation suggesting that the ability might be genetic in nature and carried on the Y chromosome. Of course then that idea is sort of dismissed pretty much by the way I decided to end the story, with Jill suddenly realizing that now she too had the ability.

As the story progressed I started thinking of more elements that played up the comedy aspect of the entire thing, most notably the part where the guys feel that they are suddenly superheroes simply because they could tell how badly women have to go to the bathroom, and then they pathetically and crazily go around in spandex uniforms trying to patrol women going to the bathroom.

I decided that in the end I would have Jill eventually accept the new situation and try to enjoy it and I thought that it should climax at one type of big event, so I chose that I would end it had a huge festival where they decide to lock the bathrooms in order to make all of the women glow in the dark, which finally leads the women to rebel against the new system that men are trying to set up against them, with Jill becoming like a bladder desperation Che Guevara, which I suppose reflects a little bit of political satire which

I kept to a minimum in this story, but I couldn't resist putting a couple of jokes in there involving politics, revolution and socialism and whatnot with sort of a feminist message that women aren't going to take men's shit forever. It may not be a global revolution against the patriarchy but taking over a men's room I thought was sort of a good way to end the story.

I then thought that the very end where Jill suddenly realizes that she has the power was just the perfect way to end it and leaves the whole thing open-ended as to what might happen next. I also added that as an ending simply because I figured that after all the frustration of not having the ability that it would just be a nice way to end it, the character getting some type of satisfaction and resolution, the way I would want to if I were in a situation like this for sure!

The bonus story I conceived of as I was finishing up the last chapters of the novel where Jill was talking to her friends on the bus about the idea of what if something like this happened in the 1950s. I thought that that would actually be a pretty hilarious type of scenario to explore in a story of its own. Given the sexual repression and prudishness of the 1950s it would be funny to see how a scenario like this would play out in a more repressive and paranoid time and I also got in a lot of good satire on 1950s society in general. I also like the fact that in the end the main character is sort of a rebel who is boldly getting herself desperate to make herself more attractive and let what society thinks be damned! It might have also been interesting to set a story where this happened in the 1960s where everyone would find reading auras of desperation to be psychedelic and groovy!

The second bonus story I actually thought of a little bit later on after I had completed this whole thing and was getting it ready for publication and then I just sort of thought of this topical idea. Admittedly I was actually writing a serious novel about racism in light of the tragic George Floyd murder, and I was going to work on that but I just kind of focused on writing some of my less serious fetish work and I just sort of conceived of this story. I hope it doesn't come across as disrespectful to set a story at a protest against police brutality, but the story just came to me and it made me think of my scenario in this novel, about how if women were suddenly glowing when they were desperate that that could open women to abuse including abuse by the police and that was kind of the idea behind that story. So I hope that you enjoyed that as well. This was sort of a contemporary story that was set in the alternate world where the alternate reality of the world where women glow when they are desperate to pee. So I guess I thought of what would be happening with contemporary events if my crazy scenario happened to be in effect.

This is the reason why I will probably think of many more stories in this universe and perhaps someday will even go as far as making an entire collection of short stories set in this world, because I think this idea really does have a lot of potential beyond what I have already written. At the very least I will probably include several stories in this universe in short story anthologies involving female desperation in the future. For now I hope you enjoy these two additional short stories set in the same universe as this novel.

Certainly there are lots of other ideas that I might very well think of as far as this concept goes. I'm not saying that I will necessarily write a sequel, as I think I covered the main ideas in this one, but I could see myself setting more stories in this specific universe using this specific concept, so it's not out of the question that I will at least write more short stories for future collections that take place in a world where this ability is real. When you include a crazy speculative element like this it lets your imagination run wild and you aren't limited by the boring confines of reality, which is why outside of my fetish writings that I am mostly a writer of speculative fiction.

If you enjoyed this speculative foray into the female desperation genre, fear not, for I have several other speculative ideas that I plan on getting around to writing eventually that combine speculative fiction with a desperate need for women to use the bathroom. But those are stories for another time!

As with much of what I write this one has some autobiographical detail built in. It does have some nods to the situation in my other books (The Great Locked Ladies Room Caper and The Terrible, Horrible, No Good Very Desperate Bus Ride) since there are several scenes that are set on buses as well as parts where the ladies room is locked, both at the amusement park and the festival. But the parts that are autobiographical are that once I did go to the Bronx zoo as a little kid and there was of course a really long line from the ladies room and I was running away from bees as I am extremely terrified of bees, so I incorporated that into this story. Also the first part where they go to a local street festival, where they eat the tacos and everything, was based on the fact that there was this sort of street fair that would come to my town all the time when I was a kid and I would go there for a while and they would have games and food and stuff like that, but one thing that they consistently lacked was any type of bathrooms! So I would go there until I pretty much couldn't take it anymore and had to run home to use the bathroom. But the street fair was only a few blocks away, so it wasn't like it was a big stretch to have to run all the way home, but it was still annoying that they did not provide any bathrooms. And I have been desperate on trains before as well more than once.

I suppose that's all I have to say about the development of this novel but I hope that you enjoyed it, and I hope that you will give it a good rating on Amazon and Goodreads. I also hope that you will also do likewise for my other female desperation themed books, The Great Locked Ladies Room Caper and The Terrible, Horrible, No Good Very Desperate Bus Ride. You can see previews from this book and others, as well as lots of personal accounts of my own desperate experiences and fictional short stories about desperation and all things bathroom related at my original blog at https://desperatejill.livejournal.com/ and my new blog at https://desperatejill83.livejournal.com/.